"Interesti
she said

She tossed her head slightly. "So that's what it's like to kiss—let's see what are you?—oh, yes, a billionaire. It'll be something to tell my grandchildren."

"When you have those grandchildren," he asked, drawling the words sarcastically, "who're they going to be calling Grandad? Anybody I know?"

Mitzi clasped her hands together in the billowing folds of her skirt. "You *know* who. You saw him. We've been in love forever."

Mac ran his fingers through his hair, pushing it sharply back from his forehead. "No," he said. "Maybe you thought you loved him when you were sixteen. You don't love him now. And he doesn't love you."

Mitzi turned from him, anger flooding her with hotness. "Stick to counting your money. As a psychologist, you don't have much promise."

"As his fiancée, you don't show much promise, either. You kiss other men too damned well."

Bethany Campbell, an English major and textbook consultant, calls her writing world her "hidey-hole," that marvelous place where true love always wins out. Her hobbies include writing poetry and thinking about that little scar on Harrison Ford's chin. She laughingly admits that her husband, who produces videos and writes comedy, approves of the first one only.

Books by Bethany Campbell

Don't miss any of our special offers. Write to us at the following address for information on our newest releases.

Harlequin Reader Service
901 Fuhrmann Blvd., P.O. Box 1397, Buffalo, NY 14240
Canadian address: P.O. Box 603,
Fort Erie, Ont. L2A 5X3

DANCING SKY

Bethany Campbell

Harlequin Books

TORONTO • NEW YORK • LONDON
AMSTERDAM • PARIS • SYDNEY • HAMBURG
STOCKHOLM • ATHENS • TOKYO • MILAN

ISBN 0-373-03062-2

Harlequin Romance first edition July 1990

To my friend Rosemary Jennings,
with affection and admiration.

CHAPTER ONE

SUMMER HAD COME to Dancing Sky, and the afternoon sun shone down brilliantly. But the most handsome man in town was in a mood of deep depression and dark insecurity.

Since keeping him happy was Mitzi Eden's self-appointed job, she had her work cut out for her.

The handsome young man's name was Barry Gabler. He sat in the town's little Victorian ice-cream parlor with Mitzi and his two aunts.

"What are we going to do?" he asked helplessly. Anxiety glittered in his ice-blue eyes.

Mitzi tried to look calm and earnest. "That's what we're going to talk about."

"What good can talking do?" Barry asked. He had black hair and perfectly shaped black brows that were drawn together in a frown of worry. "Yesterday I pick up the newspaper and what do I find? Wham! My business is about to be ruined, my future's shot, and my security is precisely zero—nothing."

His Aunt Tilly gave an ineffectual little cluck of sympathy. She looked even more disturbed and powerless than he.

"Barry," Mitzi said patiently, "we're all in the same boat. We can't panic." Yet she knew how he felt. Yesterday it seemed the earth had maliciously opened up beneath them all. It wasn't fair, it wasn't right, but it was happening. They were going to have to use every ounce of their wits to save themselves.

"I'm not panicking!" Barry's voice was sharp with wounded pride. "I'm stating facts. That doesn't mean I have to *like* them."

"Nobody said you had to like them," Mitzi soothed.

"Well, I don't," Barry insisted. "Adam MacLaren's a blood-sucking old weasel. He lives half a continent away. He's never put so much as his weasely toe in Dancing Sky. But he can sit there, make a few marks on a piece of paper, and—poof!—half the town's ruined. It's like black magic."

Mitzi nodded in resigned agreement. Adam Mac-Laren's wealth and power were so great they were like some awesome form of magic. Without ever stirring from California, he was about to change both Dancing Sky and the people who lived in it, forever.

Barry looked around the room as if dissatisfied with his life. Mitzi could tell that in his present bleak mood, he even disdained the charm of the ice-cream parlor: its dainty wire furniture, its flowered wallpaper and ruffled curtains.

She wondered uneasily if he resented her as well. She reached over and tried to pat his hand. He drew it away, too caught up in turmoil to be able to accept sympathy.

Mitzi threw a brief glance at the ceiling, as if entreating heaven for patience. She was going to need it, and badly. She had seen Barry in a great many moods, but never one this horrible.

She pushed back a wayward lock of her long dark hair. It was not black, like Barry's, but a rich dark brown, tinged with auburn when the sun shone on it. Her blue eyes, flecked with green and thickly lashed, were shadowed with concern.

Smiling was usually as natural to her as breathing. Now her smile was gone. It had been missing since yesterday, when she'd heard the news about fabled old Adam MacLaren. She'd been stunned and far more agitated for Barry and his aunts than for herself.

Barry ignored her solicitude and looked with gloomy impatience at the two older women. He obviously found no comfort in their conversation.

"I hear that MacLaren's son might take charge this time—that he may be the one behind the whole thing," fretted Tilly. "Who knows? He might be worse than his father." Tilly, a fragile little woman of sixty, tended to be imaginative and emotional.

Her larger and more rational sister, Una, frowned. "I thought MacLaren and his son were estranged. Isn't the boy too young? I heard he was some sort of juvenile delinquent—very rebellious. Uncontrollable, really."

"Too young?" Tilly blinked her large hazel eyes in confusion. "He's at least thirty, I'm sure. Nobody knows much about him. He's like his father. He stays out of the public eye."

Una, musing, shook her graying head. "How can the MacLarens be so powerful, but nobody knows hardly anything about them? Are you *sure* there's only one son? I thought there were two."

"Oh, no, no, no." Tilly was emphatic. "There's just one. Old Adam MacLaren likes his privacy. And he's got money enough to make sure he keeps it. But what if it's true—and the son's even more of a pirate than the father?"

"This isn't any help," grumbled Barry. He ran a hand over his perfectly groomed hair in exasperation.

Nobody except Mitzi looked up as the door of the ice-cream parlor opened. Its bell jingled, and a cowboy entered. He was a big man, with road dust coating his clothes and a gray Stetson hat pulled down over his eyes. He kept the hat on, which in Dancing Sky was considered proper cowboy etiquette. He looked about thirty, weathered and freckled and rugged. All that showed of his hair was a pair of reddish sideburns.

His gray eyes caught Mitzi's and held them a moment. The ghost of a smile curved his mouth. His expression told her clearly that he liked what he saw.

She looked away, embarrassed. The man gave off an almost electrical charge of basic maleness, Western-style. She was not supposed to notice such things. She was unofficially engaged to Barry. A strange cowboy drifting through town should be of no more significance to her than a puff of dust on a passing wind.

The cowboy sat down at one of the spindly little tables nearby. Unlike Barry, he seemed perfectly at ease in the Victorian excesses of the ice-cream parlor and acted as if he would be at ease anywhere. He crossed his long booted legs. Once again Mitzi felt his eyes on her. It gave her an eerie feeling.

Barry Gabler's perfectly shaped mouth took on an ugly twist. "It doesn't make any difference if it's the father or son," he said, dismissing his aunts' conversation. "A MacLaren's a MacLaren. Either way they're putting one of their lousy stores in town, and I'm ruined: I hope they both rot in hell."

"Barry!" Mitzi said in shock. Tilly and Una stared at him in amazement. He was usually careful to be a model of deportment.

Today, however, he seemed almost unable to contain himself. His gaze swept the room in disgust, as if searching for someone with sense enough to understand how serious the situation was.

The cowboy gave him a mild look and touched the brim of his hat as in greeting. Barry apparently found it beneath his dignity to notice the man and ignored him. "Ruined," he repeated. Sullenness settled over him like a cloud.

Mitzi paled with embarrassment. Barry was acting badly. She had talked him into this meeting, and the idea was obviously a mistake—a bad one. She reached out to touch his hand again.

He drew it back impatiently as if rebuffing her. Mitzi felt herself blushing. She sensed that the cowboy still watched her, and the knowledge made her blush harder.

"You two are ruined, too," Barry said to Tilly and Una. His voice was edged with anger, but with a touch of panic, too. He seemed convinced nobody except himself realized the extent of the peril. "Mitzi can probably survive. The rest of us are done for. Done for."

Tilly looked at Barry in alarm. He was nephew to her and Una, but he resembled neither of them. He had thick dark hair, skin as golden as a peach and eyes the color of sapphires. Both women often joked that Barry got all the family looks. They doted on him, and Mitzi was sure his sudden harshness surprised them. Tilly looked wounded and Una looked stern.

"Don't talk like that, Barry," Tilly pleaded. "Please don't say *ruined*. It sounds so final. We can't think that."

"We don't have any choice. We're doomed. This town is doomed." He tossed his head and ran his fingers over the smooth waves of his hair again.

The cowboy now watched Barry with something akin to dislike on his rugged face, and Mitzi resented it. The man seemed as elemental as the earth or sky. He couldn't possibly understand someone as sensitive as Barry, and he had no right to judge him. When his gaze returned to Mitzi, she raised her chin and pretended not to see him.

Una eyed her nephew coolly. "All right, Barry. We're doomed—unless we think of something. So if you don't want to help, just sit and drink your coffee. Before it gets cold." A large, practical woman, she handled the business details of the dress shop that she and Tilly had owned for years.

Mitzi furtively glanced at the cowboy who was drinking his coffee with a meditative air. He looked observant and thoughtful, like a man who missed little. Once more she was almost certain he was listening to their conversation.

"Coffee?" Barry gave Una a disbelieving stare. "How can I worry about coffee? We all know what's happening. MacLaren's putting a giant discount store here. He'll put half the stores in town out of business."

"We need to talk about this," Mitzi said firmly. "The business association's going to call a special meeting. We've got to calm down, get some ideas in order—"

"Nobody can do a thing," Barry told her in rising frustration. He pushed his cup away from him so forcefully that coffee splashed the white tablecloth. Una frowned, muttered tut-tut and mopped it with a napkin.

Barry folded his arms and stared off into a corner, paying no attention to the three women. He seemed almost too agitated to talk.

"Well, we can't just *quit*," Mitzi said. "We're going to have to adjust to this—"

"Adjust?" Barry nearly yipped. "How do we adjust to being eaten alive by the MacLaren outfit? It's easy for you to say. You won't be affected as much. The rest of us are going to be swallowed up—like little fish by a great white shark.''

"Oh, don't say *that*, dear," wailed Tilly, her fragile self-control breaking. "A shark—just like in *Jaws*? That's horrible. That's terrible. It makes me feel like—like fish bait." Tears sprang into her hazel eyes.

Una elbowed her sister to hush her and forced her to take a handkerchief. Tilly hushed and dabbed her eyes. But her chin still trembled.

Impassive, the cowboy had watched the exchange between Tilly and Barry. Then he turned his attention back to Mitzi, studying her. Once more, his gray gaze jarred her. She looked away quickly, trying to think about what Barry had said.

A shark, she thought desperately. Barry was right. A shark was an apt image for Polaris Stores, Inc. An enormously successful chain of discount stores, the Polaris stores had multiplied across the country, changing the way America shopped. Adam MacLaren, the chain's founder, had become a billionaire, one of the richest men in the nation.

Lustily he had devoured his rivals, and his dominion was truly vast. Now he was closing in on Dancing Sky. Half the merchants in town, like Barry and Una and Tilly, would suffer immediately. Others would survive awhile, only eventually to be dragged under to perish. It had happened in town after town across the nation.

Sadly Mitzi watched Tilly struggling to maintain her self-control. She had known Tilly and Una all her life. Their ladies' shop had been an institution in Dancing Sky for almost forty years. She doubted that she owned one dress that Una hadn't sold her or that Tilly hadn't fussed over, taking in the waist or making sure the length was perfect.

Mitzi pushed her ice cream away, hardly touched. "We've got to get hold of ourselves and come up with a plan." She set her jaw in refusal to give up. "We have to."

Barry still wouldn't look at her. Una, however, nodded in brisk agreement. "Right."

Tilly brightened and looked at Mitzi hopefully, as if waiting to hear some wonderful plan of salvation. But Mitzi had no plan, only the determination to come up with one.

"We . . . just have to do . . . something," she finished lamely.

Looking out of the corner of her eye, she was disconcerted to see the cowboy give her a barely perceptible nod. A slight smile once more crooked his mouth. He *was* listening to them, she thought in frustration. She shot him an unfriendly look. It bounced off him as if he wore emotional armor. His faintly amused smirk did not change a whit.

"Do something? Like what?" asked Barry. His handsome mouth took on a bitter line. "I can't beat Polaris prices."

"It's true," said Tilly, tears brimming in her eyes again. "We were in Bitterroot, Iowa, visiting our cousin. It was a busy little city once. Then a Polaris store went up. Now the downtown is dead, half the stores closed. Nobody can compete with Adam MacLaren."

"Exactly." Barry nodded, as if they finally understood his point. "Look in the next county—Cottonwood City. Downtown looks like a ghost town. Everybody in competition with MacLaren gave up."

"Then we'll be different from everyone else," Mitzi insisted. Una muttered something encouraging, but Barry's eyes flashed blue fires of despair.

The cowboy gave Mitzi another suggestion of a smile, then calmly finished his coffee. She gritted her teeth. The man was starting to rattle her.

"Listen, Mitzi," Barry hissed. "You just don't understand. Polaris sells everything we sell—only cheaper. It'll drive me out of the hardware business. And Tilly and Una out of the dress business. It's that simple—face it."

The cowboy shook his head slightly and shrugged a wide, dusty shoulder, as if making some silent comment of his own.

Mitzi wished the man would leave. She tried to concentrate. She wanted to protest Barry's hopelessness, but Barry was thirty, seven years older than she, and he didn't like her to question his experience. And what he said was true: the merchants in Dancing Sky would have to fight for their lives.

She didn't want to argue with him, especially in front of his aunts—or that irritating eavesdropper, the cowboy. Mitzi had a cheerful, giving nature, and she usually deferred to Barry, who was the only person she had ever dated. For years the town had assumed the two of them belonged together and Mitzi assumed it, too. No, she didn't want to argue with Barry.

Still, the beaten look on Tilly's delicate face stirred her to speak again. "Barry, I think—" she began.

"Mitzi, get your head out of the clouds," Barry said irritably. "There are ten stores in town that Polaris will shut down right away. Another ten will hang on awhile. But one by one they'll die. You're trying to be optimistic, but you honestly don't know what you're talking about.''

Humiliated, Mitzi stared down at her dish of melted ice cream. She supposed she really didn't know. Barry was one of the people who could be shut down almost overnight by Polaris. His little hardware store was barely breaking even now.

"I, for one, am grateful for a little optimism," said Una, backing Mitzi up. "For some spirit." She squared her large jaw and gave her nephew a challenging look.

He sighed in exasperation.

Mitzi clamped her lips together so tightly they felt numb, but kept silent. She knew she would not suffer in the coming crisis as much as the others. Her father had died last year, leaving her a small motel. Its business was probably safe for the time being, although who knew what might happen eventually? The town's whole economy would change.

She told herself that Barry had every right to be downcast, pessimistic and angry. Crafty old Adam MacLaren had made a career of driving people like him into ruin.

"If MacLaren wants to put me out of business," Una said, smoothing her gray hair, "he'll have to fight. He may have lower prices, but Tilly and I should have customer loyalty after all these years."

"Ha!" Barry's voice was cheerless. "People are loyal to their wallets, Una."

Tilly gave her handsome nephew a worried look. "Well," she hazarded. "Una's right—it's wrong just to give up. Maybe someone at the meeting will come up with something."

"Ha," Barry scoffed again. He pushed his chair back and stood. "You women can sit here and fool yourselves all you want. I've got a ranch I'm trying to run—and a store. I'm not going to sit around pretending this is going to have a happy ending.''

Barry was so distraught he forgot to pay for his untouched coffee. He stalked out into the late-afternoon sunlight. The cowboy looked after him with cool appraisal before shifting his gaze back to Mitzi, one brow cocked wryly.

She looked away, swallowing hard. The man had seen Barry at his worst, but it wasn't Barry's fault; he was facing terrible pressures. A man like the cowboy couldn't begin to understand such stress.

''I thought it'd help him to talk about it,'' Mitzi apologized guiltily to Una and Tilly. ''I was wrong. He isn't ready.''

Una reached across the little table and put her hand over Mitzi's. ''Barry's ignoring an important principle—if we give up without a fight, we deserve to lose. Somebody has to stand up to MacLaren.''

''Or his son,'' Tilly said. She picked absently at the lace on the handkerchief she clenched.

''What?'' Una frowned, crooking an eyebrow at her sister.

''Or his son,'' Tilly repeated. ''It could be Mac-Laren's son behind all this. We don't really know, do we? Adam MacLaren must be getting old. It might be his son we're up against. And hardly anyone knows a thing about *him*.''

Mitzi looked at the little woman with rueful affection. ''Tilly,'' she said, ''it doesn't matter if it's the father or the son. It's the corporation we have to face. Neither of them ever has to see this place. They can just sit in their mansion and collect the profits.''

"I just hope," Tilly murmured, oblivious to Mitzi's logic, "that the son isn't worse than the father. What if he is? Goodness, you'd think one MacLaren in the world would be enough, wouldn't you?"

Mitzi slanted her mouth sardonically. "Even one MacLaren is way too many. It's as if tornadoes and droughts and coyotes weren't enough. Nature had to get really nasty and invent MacLarens."

The big cowboy gave Mitzi an amused glance as he rose to leave. Then his expression changed. The half smile faded. His eyes held hers for a long moment. It was almost as if he was trying to speak to her without words, to convey a message of the utmost seriousness. Then he raised his hand and gave her a nod as he touched it to his hat brim in a salute of farewell.

Shaken, she looked away. She was profoundly relieved when he was gone.

"MacLaren's son, you see," Tilly said, warming to her subject, "might feel that he *has* to be even more ruthless than his father—that he has to prove himself—like on this soap opera I saw..."

Mitzi tried not to smile at Tilly's fantasies. She also tried to put the cowboy's parting look out of her mind. She had too many other things to worry about, including Una and Tilly. And Barry.

She wished she could cheer Barry. She would try again. She could not afford to be bothered by the shadowy figures of Adam MacLaren or his son.

Mitzi excused herself, paid her bill and Barry's, too, and left the ice-cream parlor. It was after six, and all the shops except the ice-cream parlor and the drugstore were closed, but she knew Barry would still be around somewhere.

Mitzi paused, looking at the town square basking in the late-afternoon sunshine. Dancing Sky was easily the prettiest little city in eastern Oklahoma, one of the few with a true old-fashioned charm.

The Rambling River wound through town, and its tumbling waters nurtured a wealth of trees. When the river was low, waters from five natural springs still flowed up from deep within the earth. Even during hard summers, when most of Oklahoma was baked dry, Dancing Sky was green and leafy and dappled with shade.

In the center of the town square was a park rich with flowers. White wooden benches graced its lawn, and a statue of a pioneer woman stood on a pedestal at the garden's center.

Shops and stores lined the four streets facing the park. These were the heart of downtown Dancing Sky. With a pang Mitzi wondered if Barry's pessimism was warranted. What if all this charm truly *was* doomed? She didn't usually hate, but she felt a sudden wave of repugnance for old Adam MacLaren.

MacLaren would prosper, as he always did. But the bustling little businesses around the square would sicken and die—all so that people could shop at a Polaris store, a building as impersonal as a warehouse. There they would buy exactly the same cut-rate items people bought in stores exactly like it all around the country. She shook her head. MacLaren and his monstrous, ugly, ever-increasing stores—it was like a blight, a plague.

Mitzi squared her shoulders and headed toward Barry's hardware store. She tried the big front door, which badly needed paint. It was unlocked. She pushed it open

and stared into the shadows lengthening inside.
"Barry?"

Dust motes floated through a shaft of late sunlight.
Looking around the cluttered little store, she inhaled its
scent of wood and metal and oil.

"What? I suppose you're going to be mad at me now,
on top of everything else."

She turned and saw him, sitting moodily behind the
counter. He was slumped in an old swivel chair, his chin
on his chest. He didn't look at her. He stared out the
dusty window. The falling shadows emphasized the
perfect regularity of his features.

"I'm not mad. I came to make sure you're all right."
She was careful to keep her tone neutral. "This has been
a shock to everybody."

"You don't act shocked."

"Barry," she cajoled. She moved to the counter and
leaned on it, next to the cash register. He didn't move
or glance at her.

"Barry," she repeated. "You can't let this get you
down."

"I can't?" His voice was bitter. "Excuse me, Mitzi,
but everything seems to be turning against me. I don't
know how much more I can take."

Mitzi sighed again in pity and frustration, wishing
Barry had more confidence in himself. Sometimes his
ego was a remarkably fragile instrument.

On the surface it seemed that he should have everything. He'd had a privileged youth with private school-
ing. After college his father had bought him the
hardware store. Five years ago, when his father died,
Barry inherited a small cattle ranch and a sizable share
of oil stocks as well, an estate worth well over half a

million dollars. In addition, he was so dark and handsome he verged on being beautiful.

The truth was not nearly as rosy, and Mitzi knew it. Barry's father, Owen Gabler had been a gruff, unaffectionate self-made man, proud, selfish, suspicious and vain of his possessions. Barry had grown up convinced that people only liked him for his looks or for his father's money. Sometimes, when he was down in spirit, he'd say he was sure his father had bought him the store because he believed Barry would never survive on his own.

After Owen Gabler's death, Barry had been afraid that people would secretly compare him to his father and find him wanting. Matters and Barry's self-confidence grew steadily worse as everything Barry touched seemed to turn to dust.

The changeability of Oklahoma's complex oil business made a casualty of Owen Gabler's stock. Two years after his death it was worthless.

The beef market plunged, and the cattle ranch suffered and went into debt. Barry hated the place, but could find no one to buy it. Now the hardware store, which he disliked almost as much as the ranch, was threatened. He had not been a lucky man. Quite the reverse.

Mitzi studied his shadowy features, wishing events didn't always hit him so hard.

"I remember the first time I saw you," she offered almost shyly, trying to coax him into a better mood. "Your father'd just moved back to Dancing Sky. He'd bought this store and you were running it. I came in to buy nails for Dad. You were standing behind the counter. Do you remember?"

He didn't answer, only stared out the window, lost in his own unhappiness.

She ignored his brooding and took a deep breath before continuing. "I'll never forget. All the girls were talking about you. When I saw you—it was as if my heart flew right out of my chest. I couldn't believe it when you asked me out."

He shrugged, as if the memories were now of little consequence. He still didn't look at her. She swallowed hard, remembering the day they'd met.

She'd just turned sixteen. Her teeth were still in braces, and her eyes were still hidden behind glasses because her father couldn't afford to buy her contact lenses. He was paying off the debts created by Mitzi's mother's final illness.

Mitzi had felt unsettled and empty after her mother's death. She needed someone to love, someone to help her forget her own unhappiness. And she had never, in her short and protected life, seen a human creature as beautiful as Barry Gabler.

Wonder of wonders, Mitzi discovered that Barry liked her and actually seemed to *need* her, too.

"Do you realize that we've been going together for seven years?" She started to smile at the thought.

"I realize it, all right." He put his fist under his chin and kept staring out the window.

Her smile died. "That's a long time, Barry. So much happened. Your waiting for me to finish high school. Your father dying. Me going off to college. Then my father... If you think after all the time we've been together that I care whether or not you're still rich—"

"I care," he interrupted, almost biting the words off. "My father left me money. I've already lost most of it. Now I stand to lose it all. What have I got to offer you?

Everybody's expected us to get married for years, Mitzi, but my money just keeps sliding away from me faster and faster. I kept hoping things would get better. They didn't. Pretty soon I won't be able to provide for a cat, let alone a wife."

The way he said the word *wife* made it sound like an intolerable burden.

"All right," Mitzi said as patiently as she could. "What I'm saying is that after seven years, if you think my opinion of you rises or falls on the fate of this—this one hardware store, you've got another think coming. We've stuck together through everything else. We'll make it through this, too."

She swallowed again. He turned his gaze from the window, looked at her thoughtfully. His face was rigid with control.

"Mitzi," he said at last, "don't think I can marry you now, when your business is probably going to end up making more money than mine. I don't want to have to live off you. I've got my pride, you know. And I want a better life for us than that crumby motel could provide."

He turned his attention back to the window and stared out at the empty street.

Mitzi gripped the countertop so tightly that her knuckles went white. There it was, rankling between them again, the motel. Barry almost seemed to resent her keeping her father's motel and managing it. His attitude hurt and perplexed her.

"Barry," she said, "the point is, if you care for somebody, you stick together through good times and bad. We just happen to be going through a bad patch now."

His expression was stark and stony. "We've got to postpone getting married indefinitely. We can't even think about it. I can't marry you if you're supporting us. People would talk."

Resentment flashed deep in her eyes. She put one hand on the old brass cash register.

"I don't care what people think. And you shouldn't, either. And I didn't ask you to marry me. I just meant I want to stand by you. Like always."

"Fine," he said, sounding relieved. "As long as that's understood. You can't rush into these things."

Seven years, Mitzi thought rebelliously, *hardly qualifies as* rushing. Once they had talked vaguely of marrying when she finished college. But when her father had died, she'd had to take over the motel, and Barry's business troubles had grown so severe they avoided speaking of it at all.

Her heart sank. His bad mood had hardened him until he refused to listen to anything she said. She had come to cheer him, to give him support and affection, but there was no talking to him. None.

"I'm going home." She stood, feeling the ornate brass of the cash register cool beneath her hand.

There was a beat of silence. "I just need to be alone," Barry said. Once more he avoided looking at her.

Mitzi straightened her spine. She wheeled and marched out the door. Once outside, her shoulders sank. Slowly she walked down the deserted street to her white Toyota.

She was angry, frustrated and at the same time frightened. She'd seen Barry's bleak, funereal moods occasionally before. But this time was different. She didn't know if the difference was in him or in herself, but it was there, and it shook her. Things seemed to be changing between them since she'd graduated and her father had died. Once she had believed things could never change.

She felt slightly panicky, almost sick. Her emotions crowded around her thickly, leaving no room for her to breathe. She drove west, toward the motel, and under her breath she cursed old Adam MacLaren and all his demon spawn.

How could one grasping, secretive, reclusive old man on a distant coast cause so much pain and confusion? How could he so coldly shatter the lives of people he didn't even bother to know? She had never felt so estranged from Barry, and it was Adam MacLaren's fault.

She remembered the cowboy, listening to the conversation in the ice-cream parlor and probably judging them all harshly. The parting look he had given her still haunted her. It was as if he were giving her a warning or an invitation or both.

She narrowed her eyes against the sinking sun. Why did the cowboy disturb her so? Perhaps it was because, drifting through Dancing Sky as he was, he was free of all the ties and complexities and responsibilities that entangled Mitzi and Barry.

She envied him. He could wander through life as easy and unfettered as the western wind. Carefree. Not like her. And not like poor, unlucky Barry.

CHAPTER TWO

MITZI PULLED her car into the parking lot of the motel.

This small piece of Dancing Sky was her kingdom, humble as it was. Her grandfather had built the motel over forty years ago, a long low building of bright pink stucco. At night, a pink neon sign flashed its message to travelers: The Pink Paradise Motel Welcomes You!

Barry said that the motel's color was horrible and Mitzi should paint it, that the name was vulgar and she should change it. But Mitzi was used to the Pink Paradise the way it was, and so was the rest of the town.

She had grown up in the pink stucco house attached to the office. It was a funny little house but comfortable and homey. As she approached the office, she checked the parking lot, mentally totaling up the evening's guests.

There was a Cadillac sedan, long, sleek and black. That was unusual. People with that kind of money usually drove on and stayed in a luxury hotel in the nearest big city.

There was also a dusty Jeep with an empty horse trailer. That was not unusual. Horse trading was a fine art in Oklahoma and had many a crafty practitioner.

Other familiar vehicles lined the curb: those of salesmen and truckers whose routes brought them regularly through Dancing Sky.

Mitzi opened the screen door and entered the office. Sherry, her part-time assistant, gave her a wide-eyed look. "Mitzi, you're *never* going to believe who's here...."

She paused for effect, but Mitzi, worried, didn't notice. "I see we have the regulars. That's good. Who else? A rancher or someone?" She was thinking of the Cadillac.

"Mitzi," Sherry said excitedly, "we've got a cowboy, all right, and I should warn you, he looks a little rough. But you'll never guess who else is here—"

"I saw the horse trailer," Mitzi said, moving behind the desk. "Who's the Cadillac belong to? Don't tell me—it's Elvis. He's still alive and hiding out in Oklahoma, right?"

"Wrong." She pushed the motel's register toward Mitzi. "Look." Sherry was a round pink-cheeked woman, and her blue eyes shone with something akin to awe.

Mitzi raised one dark eyebrow. The last entry in the register was for a Tex Farleigh of Beaumont, Texas, who listed his occupation as rodeo rider.

"Sorry," she smiled. "It doesn't ring a bell." Her smile faded as she had a sudden twinge: she hoped Tex Farleigh wasn't the cowboy in the ice-cream parlor. The thought made her singularly uncomfortable.

"Not there." Sherry pointed with excitement to the line above. *"Here."*

"Adam MacLaren, Jr., Borenwick, California. Polaris Stores, Inc.," Mitzi read.

The words took a moment to sink in. Adam MacLaren? Adam MacLaren *Jr.*? Here? In Dancing Sky? In the Pink Paradise? "This can't be true."

Sherry nodded importantly. "It's him, all right. Adam MacLaren's son. I actually met him. Isn't Adam MacLaren the sixth richest man in the whole *country*? And I've actually met his *son*!"

Sherry was star struck, dazzled by the nearness of such wealth. Mitzi, never impressed by money, felt only a chill of suspicion. "What's he doing here? What's he want?"

"He just wants to get to know us. Us, here in Dancing Sky," Sherry gushed. "Just a friendly visit. Because of the new store. And he's not what you'd expect, either, Mitzi."

Friendly visit, my foot, Mitzi thought darkly. There was more to it, surely. If a MacLaren was involved, it meant money was at stake.

Oh, heavens, she thought, maybe the son was checking out the town to see if Polaris Stores, Inc. could do something even worse than usual. She had heard rumors that MacLaren schemed to open giant grocery stores to accompany his department stores. If so, the town's three grocers were going to be in deep trouble. More disaster.

Mitzi bit the corner of her lip. She should call Barry immediately. No, Barry would only get more depressed. She didn't want that. Who was always level-headed? Una. She must call Una.

"Look, Mitzi," Sherry said. "Can I go? I can't wait to tell Jeff. Adam MacLaren's son! Right here—I stood as close to him as I'm standing to you."

Oh, good grief, thought Mitzi in despair. Sherry was probably going to want to bronze the sheets MacLaren Jr. slept in.

"Yes, yes, go," she told the woman absently. Sherry's hero worship was getting on her nerves. "Only,

Sherry—'' she paused, thinking of how to put the matter delicately ''—maybe it'd be best if you don't tell anybody except Jeff. I'm not sure what will happen when word gets out.''

But Sherry was already out the door. Mitzi shook her head. She knew Sherry couldn't keep quiet. She was as excited as an impressionable child who had just met royalty.

The MacLarens practically *were* royalty, Mitzi supposed wryly. Their enormous wealth made them more powerful than many real monarchs. But why had Adam MacLaren sent his son here?

She dialed Una's house, but nobody answered. Drat, thought Mitzi, she'd forgotten that this was the women's bridge night.

She thought of calling her friend Judy Sevenstar, but Judy cared only for horses and had little interest in business. Frustrated, Mitzi stepped to the door. She stared out at the lengthening shadows. Resentment welled up within her chest. The enemy was here, boldly camped on her very doorstep.

She should go talk to him herself, tell him exactly what she thought. Could a boy so spoiled by wealth begin to realize how his father's bloated empire affected ordinary people like Una and Tilly and Barry and herself?

And, she thought uncharitably, maybe she should make it clear that she didn't enjoy playing hostess to him or anyone connected with the Polaris store enterprise. MacLaren was an odious name to her.

She opened the door, then paused, disconcerted. The Cadillac was gone. MacLaren, Jr., must have departed for supper or a few drinks.

The office suddenly seemed too small, almost smothering. She left it, glad to savor the freshness of the open air. A field stretched behind the motel, grassy and dotted with apple trees. Often she went there to think, and instinctively she headed for it now.

She strode across the narrow back lawn of the motel, past the empty swimming pool, her hands deep in the pockets of her flowered cotton skirt. The wind rustled her long hair.

She crossed a dusty little road, then scrambled up a bank thick with summer grass. But she still wore her best sandals, and their smooth soles slipped. She felt herself sliding backward.

Out of nowhere, a hand stretched to her, a strong one. Automatically she took it.

Its grasp was powerful, and she found herself hauled up the bank and standing beside a tall man in worn jeans and a dark blue shirt of Western cut. With a start she recognized the cowboy. She stood, her hand in his, staring up at him in surprise.

The old gray Stetson hat was pushed back on his head. For the first time she could see his hair, which was an unusually dark red, thick with unruly waves. His straight eyebrows were the same rusty color, as were the lashes of his gray eyes. He was tanned but freckled as well.

He had, Mitzi thought, a rather nice face. Not handsome, certainly, just *nice*—the kind of face she would have ordinarily trusted. But she remembered the way he had looked at her in the ice-cream parlor and felt a disturbing prickle of wariness.

He was even larger than she had remembered, almost burly through the shoulders and chest. She smiled up at him uneasily, embarrassed at having slipped but grateful he had caught her. "Thanks," she said.

He still held her hand. Slowly he let go. Then he bent, picked a wild white daisy blooming by the fence post and placed it in her hand. She was too surprised to refuse it. Confused she held it, twirling its cool stem nervously between her fingers.

"The pleasure," he said, touching the brim of his hat, "was all mine."

"You must be the rodeo rider," she said nervously. She wished she could drop the flower, but it might seem rude. She gave him another perfunctory smile and nodded toward the motel. "I heard you'd checked in."

He stared down at her, his craggy face slightly puzzled. "Ma'am?" he said. She liked his voice. It was easygoing, unaffected, with only the slightest drawl.

"The rodeo rider. The cowboy," she said, her smile coming a bit easier now. "You're staying at the motel—right?"

He smiled back. She suddenly wondered why she hadn't thought he was handsome. The smile did something startling to his face. It was a beautifully white smile, and it transformed his features. Laugh lines radiated from the corners of the eyes. Even the freckles somehow looked good.

Mitzi suddenly realized why she found this man so disconcerting. In a rugged and unexpected way he was attractive. Perplexed she kept twirling the flower stem. "I saw that a cowboy from Beaumont was registered," she explained. "I run that place. It was my father's."

"It's unique," he said. She could feel him watching her, and it made the back of her neck hot. "One of a kind. I like that."

She turned toward the field, looking over the barbed wire fence. "The whole town is one of a kind. And I like that," she said. With a sinking feeling she thought again of Polaris Stores. For once even the sight of the lush and grassy meadow didn't ease her heart.

A silence fell, and she felt an awkward compulsion to fill it. "I come out here sometimes to think. I like it best when a horse or two is grazing, like now." She nodded toward the field, where a sleek bay gelding browsed under the twisted branches of an apple tree.

The silence fell again. "Ah," he said in satisfaction, following her gaze. "She's a beauty, every line. Isn't that how the song goes? She's as sweet in her form as the Queen of Connemara."

The man was almost speaking poetry to her. She did not know how to reply.

"You like horses?" he asked. It was a simple question, but again she felt as if electricity tingled the back of her neck and danced down her spine.

She mumbled yes and kept staring out at the bay beneath the apple tree.

"You have a horse?"

She nodded. "He's old. I board him at my friend Judy's. He's not even any particular breed. Just a generic horse. Are you going to buy or did you just sell?"

"Ma'am?" He crossed his arms and leaned them atop the weathered fence post. She could feel that he was examining her face intently, so she didn't want to turn her face to his again. As genial as he was, he made her feel menaced, troubled.

"The horse trailer," she said, knowing she was talking too much. "I was just interested—I thought maybe you were doing a little horse trading between rodeos."

Once more he smiled. He pushed his hat back on his unruly russet waves. "I think you've got me mixed up with somebody else. And I didn't catch your name."

Mitzi brushed her hair back from her shoulder impatiently. "Sorry." She wished the big man didn't make her so uneasy. She felt ticklish all over.

Forcing herself to ignore the feeling, she thrust out her hand. "I'm Mitzi Eden. I thought you were the cowboy registered with us. Tex somebody. From Beaumont. And you'd come out back here to stretch and get some fresh air and look at the horse."

He took her proffered hand but didn't shake it. Instead he simply held it in his large callused one, gently but firmly. "That part's right," he said, looking down at her. "Nothing prettier than a field at sunset. Oh, a few things. You are. I never saw eyes that color blue before."

Mitzi stared up at him, open-mouthed in bewilderment. Was he making fun of her? She was bewildered that a large red-haired man with freckles should seem unnervingly attractive, especially when she was used to Barry, who was so handsome he should eclipse all other men.

"They're blue but they're full of green flecks," he said, still imprisoning her hand. "Your eyes. And you crinkle them up when you smile."

"I—" she stopped, realizing she had nothing to say. To her astonishment he lifted her hand that held the flower to his lips. He kissed it on the wrist, then on the knuckles.

This, she thought with a rush of something akin to panic, was no ordinary cowboy.

"The name is Mac," he said, his breath warm as fire against her hand. "Adam MacLaren, actually, but my friends call me Mac."

He watched as amazement spread over her face. Her eyes widened, her lips parted again. She felt her body stiffen. She tried to pull her hand away.

But he held her fast. He kissed her hand one last time, giving her a brief, nerve-jolting sensation. "You liked me better when you thought I was a cowboy, right?"

"Right," Mitzi said, her voice slightly choked. His size, his closeness, his touch suddenly seemed extremely dangerous.

He released her hand with a slight flourish, as though setting a bird free. He leaned on the fence post again. He pulled his Stetson hat down and glanced at her from beneath its gray brim. "No reason we can't be friends. Tell me about your horse. Had him since you were a little girl, I bet."

Mitzi's nerves felt as if they were freezing and scalding at the same time. This was the enemy, the foe. He had surprised her because he had deceived her, pretending to be what he wasn't. This was the son of the shark, the man who had frightened everyone and driven Barry into the blackest mood she had ever seen.

She took a deep, giddy breath. She tore the daisy in two and dropped it, broken, into the grass. "We don't want you here," she heard herself telling him. "Or your store. You heard us today. You were eavesdropping. Well, you heard—we don't like you, we don't like your kind. We wish you'd never heard of Dancing Sky."

He narrowed his eyes as he turned from her, staring out at the horse in the field. His mouth curved in amused cynicism. "Too bad. Because I'm here, Miss Eden. Whether you like it or not."

She stood, her hands clasped together in the folds of her skirt. The sky had turned duskier. The west was full of gold-edged clouds, and a breeze stirred the dark fall of her hair, caressed the hot curve of her cheek.

The big man, leaning, arms crossed, on the fence post, glanced at her again. But he was no longer smiling. When he didn't smile, his face could convey a stubbornness as obdurate as stone.

She realized how rude, curt and outright nasty she must have sounded. "I'm sorry," she apologized bruskly. "I didn't mean to say that. It—just came out."

"I've heard worse." His face remained impassive.

She crossed her arms self-consciously and stared out at the bay grazing in the rippling grass. "We just heard yesterday that Polaris is coming here. The merchants in town are—quite upset."

"They usually are." He gazed up at the gilded clouds stretching across the immense sky. "Have you eaten? Want to get something? We'll talk about it."

She took a step backward, feeling confused. "No. I couldn't."

He shrugged. "A man can try. What if I'd been the cowboy? Would you have said yes?"

"No." Her heart beat a perturbed tattoo. "I've got to get back to the desk. I'm sorry for what I said. But a lot of us are unhappy about what a Polaris store will do to this town."

He straightened up, hooking his thumbs on either side of his belt buckle. He ignored her remark about the store. "You're taken? I don't notice any ring."

Oh, heavens, Mitzi thought in perplexity, the man was pretending to be interested in her. No wonder the MacLaren name was synonymous with craftiness and guile. She tossed her head, trying to show that his attentions didn't affect her. "Yes. I'm taken. More or less. Good evening, Mr. MacLaren."

He cast her a measuring look. "Which? More or less? I hope it isn't that sulky, pretty-boy jackass you were with today."

Mitzi turned frosty. His estimate of Barry embarrassed and angered her. "I don't think that concerns you."

He lifted a brow slightly but said nothing. His silence was more potent than many men's speech. No emotion at all showed on his granite features. This, paradoxically, filled Mitzi with such a tumbling confusion of emotions that her only wish was to escape.

She turned from him and scrambled back down the bank. She walked as swiftly as she could to the motel's office. Her heart thudded erratically. She could feel the man's eyes on her as surely as if he were touching her.

What was he doing, anyway, traveling economy like that? Was he like a prince trying to disguise himself as a commoner? Why was he driving that dusty Jeep and pulling that battered horse trailer? And what was he doing in Dancing Sky? She was sure his presence meant something sinister, but she had been too shaken to ask.

Her pulses drummed madly, as if they were beating out a message of the most primitive warning. *Beware,* her very heartbeat seemed to say. *Beware, beware, beware.*

CHAPTER THREE

A FAMILIAR CAR, Judy Sevenstar's red Ford, stood parked before the office. Judy herself, in jeans and a yellow T-shirt, lounged in the office's pink armchair, reading a magazine. She tossed it aside when Mitzi burst in the door. She pushed her reading glasses down on her nose and gave Mitzi a mischievous grin.

"He's here, isn't he?" Judy teased. "That MacLaren man? He was at our place this afternoon. Somebody called a few days ago about boarding a horse. I never expected this—have you *seen* him?"

Judy had been Mitzi's best friend since grade school. She was a tall, slim girl with long brown hair and hazel eyes. She was part English, part Swedish, and part Cherokee Indian. She loved horses as she loved life itself, and boarded and trained them at her father's ranch.

"He's here." Mitzi crossed her arms tightly, a gesture of tension. "I met him. I also made a fool of myself. I didn't know who he was. When I found out, I'm afraid I told him what I thought of his father's whole money-grubbing enterprise."

"Whoops." Judy smiled in sympathy. "Bad move, swifty."

"Right," Mitzi answered wryly.

"You weren't expecting a MacLaren. And you weren't expecting anybody like him." She got up and moved to the soft drink machine. "This calls for a drink. I'm buying."

She dropped coins into the machine and got soft drinks for both of them.

"I thought he was a rodeo cowboy," Mitzi said, shaking her head at her folly. "What was I supposed to think? He doesn't look wealthy."

Judy's dark eyes sparkled. "I know. That's what's so great. There's something about him. He's so...so..."

"Rich?" Mitzi gave her friend a sardonic look. "So filthy, ungodly, unbelievably, unspeakably rich?"

Judy shrugged and laughed. "Well, there's that. But he doesn't look it, he doesn't act it, and he's like... like..."

"Good grief," accused Mitzi, "you're as bad as Sherry. He's got you addled, too."

"He does not," Judy looked at the diamond on her left hand. "I'm true to Don. I just wish he'd finish medical school before the century's over. In the meantime, here's this man who's so...so..."

Mitzi looked at her friend with amused disgust. "He's so *what*, for heaven's sake? One measly millionaire comes along, and suddenly the cat's got your tongue?"

"Billionaire," Judy corrected, leaning an elbow on the counter. "All right, how's this? He gives you the feeling he's rock solid. That he's seen it all and done it all and if you need him, you can count on him. How's that?"

Judy's words struck Mitzi as being eerily accurate, but she wasn't sure they were. Mac MacLaren's air of dependability could be a carefully cultivated illusion.

"Who knows?" Mitzi returned broodily. "I've heard his father's on old devil who can make you trust him—right up to the moment he cuts your throat."

"That's his father, not him. He seems like a very nice guy. He told Dad he just came here to look the place over."

Mitzi felt her body stiffen in uneasiness again. "I think he's up to something. I've heard rumors that the MacLarens are expanding. Getting into groceries, a bunch of other stuff."

"A plot? I doubt it. He seems honest."

"Things aren't always what they seem." Mitzi's mouth took on an unhappy curve. "The MacLarens could be experimenting with Dancing Sky. Seeing exactly how much business they can take over."

"Oh, Mitzi," Judy said, crossing her booted legs, "don't be silly. You sound like it's the days of range wars again."

"These are modern range wars. The question is still the same. Who controls the territory?"

Judy shrugged. "*That* question was going on before the Indian Wars. It'll always go on. Some of my ancestors lost this land. Others won it. Maybe it all works out in the end."

Mitzi, still shaken, couldn't be as philosophical. "Not for the losers."

Judy merely adjusted her glasses and rummaged through the depths of her fringed purse. "Wait till you see this man's horse. I took some pictures. You won't *believe* this animal."

"Now it's clear," Mitzi said, finally smiling a bit. "It's his horse that impressed you. I should have known."

"Listen—" Judy began. But the crunch of gravel outside and the creaking open of the screen door interrupted her.

A small, bandy-legged man in jeans and an immense white Stetson hat stood in the doorway. His hat band was ornamented with enough feathers to reconstruct a small pheasant, and his silver belt buckle was as large as a saucer. He was drunk.

Oh, no, Mitzi thought sickly. She'd had enough catastrophe for one day. The little man swaggered toward them. He looked with interest at Judy, then with even greater interest at Mitzi.

"Ladies," he said, swinging his shoulders importantly, "you just got lucky. I'm here to make your evenin'. Tex Farleigh's my name, rodeo's my game. I can ride a bull, wrestle a steer, rope a calf and make a lady so happy she'll grin all the next day. And who might you pretty things be?"

Judy turned up her nose. "We're not interested, cowboy. Leave. Go away."

"Steady," Mitzi warned her out of the corner of her mouth. "This is one of our distinguished paying guests."

The small florid man looked at Judy with an air of insult. "You're my second choice anyway, honeybunch. You're too skinny. I like 'em with a curve or two."

He leaned across the counter and tried to seize Mitzi's arm. She dodged him. "What's your name, sweet thing?" he demanded.

"Mr. Farleigh," Mitzi replied with elaborate calm, "I'm busy. And you need to move your car. Your Cadillac is crossways in the drive. I can see it from here. Somebody might hit it."

"Don't worry about the car, darlin'," he said, trying to move behind the counter to pursue her. "There's more where that one came from."

Judy temporarily blocked his way. "Look, mister, you'd better back off. She has a big mean boyfriend. Big and mean and jealous."

The swaggering little cowboy was not deterred. He squinted at Mitzi's conspicuously bare left hand. "She ain't got no ring. If she's got such a big, mean, bodacious boyfriend, why ain't he here?"

He pushed roughly past Judy, who looked suddenly frightened.

"He is here." The voice was deep and easy. Mac stood in the doorway. One corner of his mouth turned up slightly. "The lady's taken, friend. I'd appreciate your leaving now. And be sure to move the Cadillac."

The cowboy was small but pugnacious. He looked up at Mac MacLaren, scowling blearily. "The bigger they are, the harder they fall. I can whip five guys your size, one hand behind my back."

Mac took off his hat and sighed. The lamplight glinted on his fiery hair. "I imagine you're right, friend. So let's not fight. Fighting's not the intelligent way to settle differences. And you're obviously an intelligent man."

The cowboy suppressed a slight belch and tried to look dignified. He put his hands on his hips and looked up at Mac, who stood a full foot taller. "That's right," he said, somewhat mollified. "I'm an intelligent man. I most certainly the hell am."

"Then let's act like gentlemen. Let the lady decide." He turned to Mitzi. He gave her a mild version of the smile that she had found devastating before. "Who's your fellow, sugar?"

Mitzi looked at him, then at the bandy-legged rodeo rider, who swayed slightly on his high-heeled boots. She turned her gaze helplessly back to Mac. "You are." She swallowed hard.

"And who did you aim to spend the evening with?" He kept his smile the same, at once both innocent and provocative.

Mitzi swallowed harder. The little man scowled up at Mac, as if still wondering whether to start a fight.

"I said, sweetheart," Mac coaxed, "who'd you plan to spend the evening with?"

Mitzi leaned back against the cash register for support. "With you." Her voice sounded weak in her ears.

"And who," Mac asked, all purring sweetness, "is the man you love with all your heart and soul? Darling?"

Mitzi found it hard to breathe evenly. "You are."

Mac put his hand on the little man's shoulder. "Friend, I believe this woman has just gone and got used to me. Fine man like you, though, can get plenty of ladies. Wouldn't hurt for you to leave this one for me. And the other one for her fellow. She's wearing that ring, after all." He nodded toward Judy, whose eyes were enormous behind her glasses.

Tex Farleigh stared up at Mac suspiciously. He seemed uncertain what to do next.

"Tell you what," Mac said smoothly. "To show there're no hard feelings, how about a drink? I've got a bottle of bourbon. What say we go to your room and split it?"

Tex Farleigh frowned, thinking hard. "All right," he said. "I guess." He looked at both women, who stared back at him in apprehension. "They're both awful tall anyway," he complained. "Don't know what they been puttin' in girls' vitamins nowadays, make 'em so tall. They grow up like weeds.''

With Mac's arm around his shoulder, Tex Farleigh allowed himself to be steered, staggering slightly, out of the office.

Mitzi and Judy stood tensed.

"Oh!" Judy gasped. She threw herself down in the chair and put her hand over her heart. "I thought we were going to have to subdue the little rodent by force."

"So did I." Mitzi was cold all over and knew she must be pale. "I was scared," she admitted.

"I was *petrified*," Judy said. "He got aggressive. Thank heaven for the MacLaren man. What are you doing?"

Mitzi picked up the phone. Her hands shook slightly. "Calling Barry. The world's out of control. I need re-inforcements."

Judy glanced significantly at the door through which Mac had left. "I think you have mighty fine reinforcements already. I think he's got a gleam in his eye for you."

Mitzi didn't bother to reply. She listened to the ring-ing of Barry's phone.

At last he answered. "Hello." It sounded more like a lamentation than greeting.

"Barry, it's Mitzi." She tried to keep her voice from trembling. "All sorts of things are happening—"

"Mitzi, I'd like to help you, but you don't under-stand. I've got serious troubles on my hands. You've got to realize how bad this Polaris thing is. If the hard-ware business doesn't kill me, then this damn ranch will. Beef prices just fell again, I've got a heifer with a bro-ken leg, and I still can't find a decent foreman."

Barry, please! she wanted to scream. Instead she tried to soothe him before asking for his help. "I'm sorry about the beef prices. I'm sorry about the heifer. And the foreman, too. But I wish you'd come over. A drunk, one of the guests, just got fresh with Judy and me. Everything's all right now, but—"

"If everything's all right, then you don't really need me, do you, Mitzi?" Barry sounded weary, like a parent tired of explaining something to a child.

"Well, it's all right now, but—" Mitzi said "—but there are other—"

Barry interrupted her. "Mitz, I'd like to help you, but I just told you. I'm up to my neck in my own problems. I've got that heifer to tend to. Now can't you just be a good girl and calm down?"

Mitzi frowned, hurt. "Barry, you've got to listen—"

"Honey, I know I've been in a bad mood, but this Polaris thing is serious. It affects our whole life. You've got to just let me think, all right?"

"Barry—" she almost wailed.

"Mitzi?" His voice had gone stern. "Did you hear what I said?"

"Yes, I heard you." She wondered why he so steadfastly refused, in his turn, to hear her. She needed to talk to him about Mac MacLaren. It suddenly seemed important and necessary that Barry be the one she could turn to.

"Mitzi," he said, "I'll call you tomorrow. I just can't deal with anything extra right now. You understand— you always understand. All right?"

She felt a knot of coldness, heavy as a stone, form in her chest. "All right." She tried to keep emotion out of her voice. "Call me when you feel up to it."

He didn't notice her change of tone. "Yeah," he said rather absently and hung up.

She set down the receiver, her heart hammering. Then she raised her face and met Judy's searching eyes.

Judy took off her glasses and gave her friend a wary look. "I couldn't help hearing. What's his problem now? Why do you always have to be the strong one? Why don't you ever get to lean on him?"

Mitzi exhaled in frustration, blowing an unruly tendril of hair from her eyes. "Barry hasn't got it easy right now." She tried to ignore the fact that she had made this same excuse for Barry so many times it was beginning to sound mechanical, even to her.

"Stop," Judy ordered, putting her hands over her ears. "My heart will break. Mitzi, I swear, this used to be interesting—we'd sit around for hours, talking about poor Barry, his problems and his bad luck. But, frankly, lately—"

Mitzi set her mouth stubbornly. "I don't want to talk about it." It was disloyal of her to think unkindly of Barry, and even worse to let Judy say such things.

"All right." Judy sighed and shook her head. "I should have known better. Let's talk about the weather. Nice weather we're having. Do we need rain? I think we need a little rain. What do you think? Do you think we need a little rain?"

Both looked up as they heard the scuff of boots on the gravel outside. Mitzi hoped the drunken cowboy wasn't about to reappear.

She didn't know whether to be relieved or disturbed when Mac stepped into the office. His face had an ironic cast. "Your guest's asleep. He should be out for the night. I moved his car, and here're his keys, just in case.

You can give them back in the morning. Tell him that friends don't let friends drive drunk."

He tossed the keys onto the counter. His Stetson hat was gone. His hair, thick and glinting like dark fire, fell over his forehead. The muscles of his upper arms strained the fabric of his shirtsleeves.

"Thanks." She took the keys and put them in the safe under the counter.

"You're welcome."

The room went awkwardly silent. Mac rubbed his chin thoughtfully. He studied Mitzi, and Mitzi studied the floor. Judy Sevenstar watched both of them over the rims of her glasses. Her expression grew mischievous again.

"Mitzi and I were just talking about rain, Mr. MacLaren. Do you think we need rain?"

He gave her a wry, sideways look, then returned his attention to Mitzi. Amusement played at the corners of his mouth. "Couldn't say. I only know that our friend Tex doesn't hold his liquor well. But he can probably hold a grudge. If he thinks I lied, he'll run me down with that Cadillac. So, Miss Eden, I think you should reconsider. Go out with me. As an act of mercy. How about dinner?"

Mitzi felt excitement mingle with alarm. What did Mac think he was doing? Undermining his enemy's morale with polite invitations? His glances seemed friendly, but they pulsed with an undercurrent of danger.

"I can't go anywhere. I have to stay here," she insisted.

"No, you don't," Judy offered so instantly that Mitzi almost jumped in surprise. "I'll watch the place. It's no big deal. You and I have done it a hundred times."

Mitzi gave her friend a sharp look of warning. "No. I can't—"

"Yes, you can," Judy interrupted, a look of determination settling over her face. "I owe you a favor anyway. You drove me to Tulsa last week. So go ahead. Run along."

Mitzi stared furiously at Judy, but her friend ignored her and began fanning through her magazine. "I *can't*," Mitzi repeated through clenched teeth.

Judy didn't look up. She flipped a page. "I'll be fine. I'll phone Milo. He'll come keep me company. I was coming to town to see him anyway."

Mitzi gritted her teeth harder. Judy glanced up at Mac, her face all friendly innocence. "Milo's my brother. He's a deputy. We were going to spend the evening together anyway. I couldn't be in safer hands. So enjoy yourselves, you two."

You traitor, Mitzi thought bleakly.

"Then it's settled." Mac leaned lazily against the counter, smiling. "Where's the best place to eat?"

Judy shrugged. "About halfway to Talequah. A place called Buffalo Bill's. Great steaks. Great catfish. Great desserts."

Mitzi looked from Mac to Judy and back to Mac. "I can't go." Her voice almost faltered.

"What's the matter?" Mac asked. "You're not married. Are you engaged?"

"Yes," Mitzi answered in panic.

"No, she's not." Judy's voice was cool in contrast. "Not yet. Not by a country mile."

Mac raised one eyebrow. His gaze still glittered on Mitzi. His smile was skeptical. "Are you engaged? Yes or no?"

"Well," Mitzi admitted nervously. "No. Not exactly."

"Good." He stepped behind the counter and held his hand out to her.

She stared at it. It was strong, tanned and freckled. She remembered its warmth and its power.

A thousand thoughts jumbled together in her mind, whirling like leaves in a sudden gale. If she went with Mac MacLaren, he might give her a few answers about why he was there, about what Polaris was going to do in Dancing Sky.

Yet she shouldn't go. No matter what her motives, Barry would be profoundly wounded. Or would he be angry if she didn't go, offended that she didn't take advantage of the opportunity?

She had no idea. She did not begin to understand why she let her eyes stay fastened, as if hypnotized, on Mac MacLaren's homely-handsome face. Nor did she understand why she raised her hand and put it tentatively in his large one.

But take his hand she did. It pulsed with vitality against her own. His fingers closed around hers.

"Good," he said again. "Good."

He drew her to his side. He looked down at her, giving her a one-cornered smile. Without another word he led her off into the starry night.

CHAPTER FOUR

"I'M NOT GOING halfway to Talequah," Mitzi warned Mac as he settled beside her in the Jeep. "I refuse. We can pick up some sandwiches and eat in the park. I want to be home in an hour. What if that cowboy wakes up? I can't leave Judy."

"Make it two hours," he replied easily. "He won't wake up. I told you, he can't hold his liquor. All it took was one more drink to put him out. Besides, she's calling her brother."

"One hour." Mitzi's tone was emphatic. "Then I want to go home. I'm not a puppet, and you can't make me dance. Just because you're a trillionaire—"

He backed up then eased the Jeep out of the parking lot and onto the highway. "Just a billionaire." Satire laced his tone. "Sorry."

"All right," Mitzi muttered, staring out the window at the star-strewn sky. "Billionaire. Either way I'm not impressed."

"Nobody asked you to be. You're not the type it would impress, anyway. It's more embarrassing than anything else." He glanced in the rearview mirror, then signaled for a turn. "I've got to stop at the service station. Drop off this horse trailer. Something's wrong with one of the wheels."

Mitzi gave him a suspicious glance. In the semidarkness she could see that he had a craggy profile, and his hair tended to be unruly, to look windblown even when it wasn't windy.

"What's so embarrassing about being rich?" she asked sarcastically. "If money bothers you, I know plenty of people who'd love to take it off your hands."

He pulled into the service station's island of light. "One thing that's embarrassing is that I have to borrow ten dollars from you." He shut off the ignition. "Fifteen would be even better. Have you got it?"

"What?" Mitzi cried, staring at him in disbelief. "You want to borrow money from me? From *me*?"

He turned, raising one auburn brow philosophically. "Right. The only cash I have right now is a five-hundred-dollar bill. And two quarters and a dime. No sandwich place is going to cash a five-hundred-dollar bill. So—would you lend me ten or fifteen dollars?"

He gave her a mocking smile and got out of the Jeep. Mitzi sputtered something unintelligible but began fumbling through her purse. Going out with a billionaire wasn't exactly what she would have imagined. First, he was dropping off an extremely smelly horse trailer. Now he was borrowing money.

By the time the trailer was unhitched, she had found a small trove of dollar bills and loose coins. "Fourteen dollars and nineteen cents," she said, handing him the money as he got in. "And I want a receipt. I've heard rich people always forget to pay their debts."

He took the money and stuffed it unceremoniously into the back pocket of his jeans. "Okay, with my change, we've got fourteen dollars and seventy-nine cents. Where can we get the best meal on that? And a bottle of wine?"

"I mean it," Mitzi replied, rather pettily. "I want a receipt. What are you, one of those tightwads who wears old clothes because you hate to spend money and tries to mooch free meals?''

His lip curled in derision. He reached into the pocket of his jeans again and withdrew a crumpled piece of paper. Taking a pen from the dashboard, he scribbled something on it. He handed it to her. "Receipt."

Mitzi gasped. He had handed her the five-hundred-dollar bill. Across it, he had written in large black letters, "I.O.U. $14.19—M. MacLaren."

"I can't take this," she protested, practically recoiling from the money. "I won't carry around this much money. Here—take this immediately!"

He paused. He put the Jeep into gear, then turned and looked at her. "Look," he said, one corner of his mouth turning up and one down. "Make up your mind. You want a receipt or not?"

Mitzi held the bill out to him gingerly. "Not this. This is ridiculous. What are you, one of those people who go around flaunting money and lighting cigars with hundred-dollar bills?"

"I'm apparently one of those people who can't win," he said between his teeth. "First you call me a tight-wad, then a spendthrift. I'm damned if I do and damned if I don't. You asked for a receipt. I gave you one."

"Take it, take it." Mitzi waved the money at him nervously.

"Then all I can give you is my word. Is my word worth fourteen dollars?"

"Yes. Yes. Now take this thing."

He took the money and stuffed it into his back pocket again. He eased into the town's light traffic once again. "Now. Where do we get something to eat?"

Disconcerted, Mitzi told him the best fast food in town came from Bubba's Drive-Thru Burger Palace. Bubba's little restaurant was humble but bustling, one of the hubs of Dancing Sky's limited nightlife. Mitzi saw several cars she recognized and slumped down in the seat of the Jeep.

"What's wrong?" Mac gave her a speculative glance. "Don't you want to be seen with me?"

"No, I don't," Mitzi said honestly and slouched lower still. "I told you back at the motel, I'm engaged—practically. People might misunderstand."

He lifted one shoulder and set his jaw skeptically. "Then why'd you come with me? You could have said no. What's the matter? You and your so-called fiancé didn't seem to be getting along so well today. Having a tiff? Is that why you're here?"

Mitzi shrugged back, sinking still more deeply into the seat. Mac's questions were fair but disconcerting. "He hasn't been the easiest person in the world to be around lately." She glanced up at Mac's profile, his hair with its rebellious forelock. "And it's your fault," she added, wanting to shift the guilt so it was more evenly distributed.

"My fault? Oh. The Polaris store. It'll affect him. What's he do?"

"He runs a few cattle on his ranch. But he also owns the hardware store." She glanced nervously about Bubba's parking lot, hoping no one would recognize her.

"Hardware store?" Mac suppressed a snort of derisive laughter. "That's his? Hasn't done much with it, has he? Hell, anybody could put him out of business."

"It may not look like much to you, but at least he made it on his own. He didn't inherit it from his father." She bit her lip, for she had spoken without thinking. In truth, Barry hadn't made anything on his own. His father had given him the store and left him the ranch, and Barry, through no fault of his own, seemed destined to lose both.

"And where'd you get that motel?" She heard a note of lazy challenge in the question. "Built it up from nothing, did you?"

Her mouth crooked with frustration. Mac MacLaren was out of her league in every way, and she could never say the right thing to him.

"I said where'd that motel come from? Hammer it together yourself? Hmm—it's awfully quiet in here."

"I inherited it," she admitted. "But my inheritance doesn't compare with yours."

"Then don't compare them," he offered, cutting her off. "You're the one who keeps talking about money, not me."

She felt her face grow hot. She tried to slip further down in the seat and found it was impossible without doing contortions. She was grateful when their turn came at the drive-through window and Mac had to turn his attention to counting out the dollar bills and quarters and dimes and pennies to the attendant.

"Here," he said, handing her the warm paper sack that contained their sandwiches. "And don't worry. I'll grab a bottle of wine, then take you someplace quiet. Nobody'll see you consorting with the enemy. Or is it your boyfriend that worries you?"

"Both." She shifted uncomfortably and settled the sack on her lap.

She didn't want to be seen with Mac MacLaren. He truly was the enemy, and Barry might misunderstand and be hurt. She had no wish to hurt Barry, now or ever. Yet being with Mac bothered her in other ways, ways she didn't understand and didn't want to. She shouldn't have come with him. It was a terrible mistake.

"It'll be all right," he assured her. There was confidence in his voice, but a certain weariness, as well. "I'll take care of you. You'll be fine."

She glanced at him. His face had an impassive, shuttered look. A shame—the thought came unbidden—because his face wasn't meant to be impassive. Great wealth, she realized, must isolate a person terribly. The man beside her, she recognized, must live in a peculiar and impenetrable solitude.

"What's the matter?" he asked. "I told you I'd take you where you wouldn't be seen. Don't you believe that, either?"

She turned to gaze out the window at the glittering stars. "I believe you. I just don't understand why you want me with you. I'm not very good company. At least not around you."

The only answer he gave her was silence, as if he didn't know why he wanted her there, either.

He bought the wine, then drove her to a spot she hadn't visited since her teens. It was a deserted old one-room school house, empty for almost thirty years.

It stood in a grove of hickory trees on a high hill overlooking the Rambling River. The road to it was seldom used these days. She wondered how Mac had found it. She and Judy had sometimes ridden their horses to this place during their high school years.

Time had not been kind to the old building. Its windows were boarded over, and the last vestiges of paint had weathered away, leaving the old wood looking silvery in the moonlight.

"How'd you ever find this place?" she asked, truly curious.

He gave her a cryptic smile as he parked. He got out and opened her door.

"It's a hobby," he said, helping her out of the vehicle. "Taking the back road, the odd way, the different route. Not much left of the building, but it's a nice spot."

The night wind tossed her hair, played with her skirt. The stars seemed even brighter on the hill, the moon lower and brighter. The wind creaked in the hickory trees and rustled the fragrant grasses.

Mitzi breathed deeply. She had forgotten how she had always loved this spot. She had never seen it at night. It seemed enchanted, otherworldly.

He nodded toward the old school building. "We can sit on the stairs. I know you're going to ask questions. I hate questions, but if I have to answer them, I might as well have some scenery to look at."

"You must like scenery." She remembered him watching the sun set over the field.

"I should. I've seen enough. Sit down." He stared out into the darkness, studying the view a moment. Then he took out a pocket knife and, using its corkscrew, opened the wine. He poured it into two plastic glasses he had bought.

Mitzi sat beside him. She couldn't help smiling.

"What's the matter?" he asked, handing her a glass of wine.

She looked at the wine sparkling in its plastic glass. She held it toward him as if in a toast. "I never thought I'd have dinner with the son of a millionaire—excuse me—billionaire. And I never thought it would be like this."

He touched his glass to hers. The plastic clicked. "Here's to the simple life. And to listening to the whip-poorwills while we eat. Now do you wish you'd opted for a good steak somewhere east of Talequah?"

"No," she said and meant it. "Anybody can eat in a restaurant. I'd rather be here."

"With me? Or with your almost-fiancé?"

She had been feeling almost comfortable with him, but now was taken aback. It took her a moment to find her voice. "With him, of course," she said primly.

Mac gazed out at the dark hills. "And what if I'd swept you off somewhere better than this—say chartered a jet and flown you to some seaside restaurant on the Gulf. Dropped pearls in your champagne and had violins play in your ear?"

Mitzi looked at him suspiciously. Was that the sort of thing he usually did when he took a woman out? Was this humble picnic on a moonlit hill some sort of comic novelty for him? Something he would laugh about?

She made her answer tart. "If you were going to spend that much money, I'd just as soon you'd buy me new garbage cans for the Pink Paradise. Mine are all dented."

"I offer you romance, and you ask for garbage cans? What planet did you come from?" He shook his head. A breeze came up, riffling the unruly thickness of his hair.

Mitzi nibbled at her hamburger self-consciously. "I'm not looking for romance. Not with you. The only reason I came is . . ." she paused, wondering if she were about to tell the truth.

"Yes?" The moonlight silvered his features, made them sterner somehow.

"Because I want some answers. What are you doing in Dancing Sky? It can't be standard procedure for one of the great MacLarens to show up every time a new Polaris store goes up. You'd never see home."

He didn't look at her. He stared out at the stars. "Every year I need to represent my father more. Someday I'll run the whole business. I wanted to see the process of a store going up—what goes on from the first step. That's all."

Mitzi's suspicion increased. His words sounded too pat, almost rehearsed. "That has the ring of an official statement. But not necessarily of the truth."

He turned, looking down into her eyes. He wasn't smiling, and again she was aware of how the moonlight made his features seem harder. "It is an official statement. And as much of the truth as I can tell you. Right now."

Mitzi's mind raced, too many thoughts spinning through it too swiftly. The man beside her offered nothing but contradictions. Like many big men he bore himself with surprising gentleness. Yet she sensed an almost frightening toughness beneath the surface. She reminded herself that he was the enemy. His presence posed a threat to Barry and Tilly and Una and herself.

"Do you know what a Polaris store will do to this town?" she asked.

"I have a good idea."

His coolness angered her. "Well," she told him with asperity, "we don't want it to happen. You'll ruin this town. And the people in it."

He laughed. "Don't be naive. Most people will be better off. You're worried about yourself. Yourself and a few privileged friends."

His arrogance astounded her. She gave him a scath-
ing look. "Privileged friends? How do you have the
gall—you with this massive *fortune*—to sit there and
call me and my friends privileged?"

"Anybody with his own business is privileged." He'd
finished the last of his sandwich, wiped his hands clean
and poured himself another glass of wine. "It's an opportunity. It's also a responsibility. I've got the same
opportunity and the same responsibility. It's a question of size. When I act, I act for thousands. It makes
me careful. You'd probably say ruthless."

Mitzi looked at the stubborn set of his jaw and felt
her own stubbornness rising. "Ruthless is too mild.
Don't you care what your stupid store will do to people?"

He reached out. He put his hand under her chin and
tipped her face up slightly, so she had to look directly
into his eyes. She held herself rigid, refusing to show
reaction.

"Most people," he said, an edge in his voice, "will
see it as a godsend. I thought maybe you'd be honest
enough to admit it. I was wrong. Sorry. Still, you've got
lovely eyes."

"My eyes have nothing to do with the issue." She
hated the quaver she heard in her voice. Although his
hand beneath her chin was gentle, his touch imprisoned her as surely as chains. She could not turn her gaze
from his.

"They're just a different issue," he suggested. His
face moved closer to hers, and for the first time she noticed the sculpted curve of his lips.

Abruptly she forced herself to turn her face from his.
She shifted farther away from him on the stair. "The
issue," she said, wondering why it was so hard to

breathe, "is business. I came to talk it, not to swoon at your feet. I have friends your store will hurt. I don't like that."

He reached out and took her hand, making her face him again. "Look me in the eye and tell me that Polaris will do more harm than good here."

His face was unyielding yet not cruel. She could not fathom his expression, but it was disturbingly intent. "It will." She tossed her head in defiance. "Far more."

She tried to shake off his grasp, but he held her fast.

"Steady. I want you to listen. Polaris will benefit this town."

Mitzi gave a short laugh of derision.

He bent so that his eyes were level with hers. "Look. That woman working for you—the little roly-poly one. What's her name?"

"Sherry," Mitzi answered, glaring at him. All her pulses seemed to be leaping, and she wondered if he could feel them dancing.

"Sherry," he repeated, his fingers inexorable around hers. "And do you hire Sherry full-time?"

"No." She hoped the disdain in her voice would hide how irregular her breath had become. "I can't afford to."

"I could. And pay her more." He smiled with satisfaction.

She said nothing, but her eyes flashed.

"I could offer her more opportunity," he added, undeterred by her hostility. "Promote her. Where can she go, working for you? Nowhere. I can give her extra benefits. What can you give her? Nothing. So who's Sherry better off with—me?—or you?"

Mitzi refused to give him the satisfaction of a direct answer. "Sherry's only one person."

"Is she married? What's her husband do? Do they have kids?" Mac probed.

Mitzi made an impatient face. "She's married to a teacher. They have two children. So what?"

"They have to stretch money as far as they can?" he demanded.

"Everybody does. Again—so what?" She wished he would release her hand. His touch was starting to make her slightly dizzy.

Instead his grip tightened. "I'll tell you what. Everybody's money stretches furthest at Polaris. Rethink it, Mitzi. Who does the store harm? Nobody. Except a few merchants who won't adapt to competition."

A breeze sprang up, ruffling his already unruly hair. The moonlight shone starkly on his cheekbones. "All right," she admitted, impatience etched on her face. She edged back slightly. His face was too close to hers, and his nearness did things to her that frightened her. A foreign excitement spun through her blood. She tried to keep her mind on business and think clearly.

"All right," she said, her breath uneven. "But that's just money. Look at everything else that's lost."

"What's lost?" he scoffed. He stared at their linked hands. He traced his thumb slowly across the inside of her wrist. "Profits of a few local yokels? That's just money, too, isn't it?"

Mitzi's body stiffened. Her hand went rigid in his. "We are not," she informed him, "*yokels*. Not being a billionaire doesn't make someone a *yokel*. You know what I mean—traditions are lost. Beauty is lost. Your stores look like—like warehouses. They're big and impersonal. They look like robots designed them for robots to shop in."

She tried to jerk free from his grasp. Deftly he kept her imprisoned. "I said I want you to listen," he warned, his voice soft but slightly dangerous. "So listen. The stores are efficient. They keep costs down. That's not criminal."

His logic assailed her mind, just as his nearness attacked her senses. Mitzi blinked back tears of frustration. She felt cornered and disoriented.

"You're the one who won't listen," she accused. "You put that store here, and what happens to people like Tilly and Una—the women who run the dress shop? They're like part of the heartbeat of this town."

She stopped. She thought of the other people whose businesses had always seemed a part of Dancing Sky. The elderly face of Lloyd Beecham suddenly floated into her mind, haunting her. Could Mac MacLaren ever understand about someone like Lloyd? Could she make him understand? She took a deep breath.

"There's a man named Lloyd. He's been the town druggist ever since I can remember. He's getting old and tired—how can he compete against you? You'll destroy him—but you won't admit it. You just hide behind your smug arguments."

Mac's face remained implacable. "He can survive if he adjusts. So can Tilly and Una. Adaption is the key, Mitzi. The smart survive."

She shook her head, disconcerted by both his words and his touch. His hand felt like a band of warm steel around her wrist.

"You don't want to believe it, do you?" He bent closer, as if exacting an answer.

"Let go," she said, defeat in her voice. She knew there were arguments she should marshall against him, but she was too perplexed to think of them.

He did not release her. "I don't have to be the enemy."

She shook her head again. "Yes. You're the enemy, all right. Get away from me—you don't have any right to touch me."

He stood up, his hand still firmly grasping hers. He drew her up to stand beside him. "I know I don't have any right," he said, gazing down at her. "But I have wants. Like anybody else. And I want to touch you."

Her heart did something painful within her chest. She stared up at his shadowy face, ringed by stars. She could not speak.

"You know why I kissed your hand when we met?" His voice was low.

"No," she breathed, turning her face away. She stared down at the shadowy grass swaying in the moonlight. He had taken her other hand now, lacing his fingers through hers. "You shouldn't have done that, either."

He drew closer to her, but still she refused to look at him. His lips were so near her ear that his breath fluttered her dark hair. "I kissed your hand because I wanted to kiss your mouth. Your beautiful mouth that crooks one way when you're happy and another when you're sad. I didn't think I'd ever get the chance. So I kissed your hand."

He raised both her hands. He bent his head and kissed them again, first the left, then the right.

"Stop." She tried to step away, to escape what he was doing to her. But her resistance was weak, benumbed. She made the mistake of looking up at him again. His rugged face, so near her own, made her feel trembly and strange. "Stop..." The word came out as an ineffectual quaver.

"Make me stop," he whispered harshly. He pulled her into his arms, and his mouth bore down on hers.

He kissed her until she was so warmly dizzied by it that it seemed the stars had changed their ancient paths and danced around the two of them.

"Make me stop." He breathed the words tersely against her lips. Then he kissed her again.

She found herself putting her arms around his neck, unable to stop even herself.

CHAPTER FIVE

SOMEWHERE in the rustling trees, a hoot owl called. Mitzi, wrapped in the warmth of Mac's arms, barely heard its plaintive sound.

Her heart shook within her chest. The ground seemed to sway beneath her feet. She was afraid to open her eyes, because she was sure that Mac had performed some black magic on ordinary nature. The dark hills no longer seemed solid or enduring. The only real thing in the world was the touch of Mac MacLaren.

Even as his lips drew back from hers for a moment, he pulled her nearer, so that her body was pressed more intimately against his, wrapped more irresistibly in his embrace.

"Hey," he said softly, gazing down at her, his face intent. "You're trembling. You're shaking like a little leaf. Why?"

Mitzi, frightened by her own emotions, kept her eyes closed. She felt as if she were drowning in forbidden pleasures and temptations. She trembled even harder.

Mac looked at the shadows the moonlight cast of her long lashes against her cheek, at the curve of her lips silvered in its light. Desire and tenderness flooded through him in a rush, mingling like two swift rivers.

If she opened those blue eyes and looked up at him, he wondered if he'd fall into her gaze, moonstruck and lost, like a man bewitched. Or, he thought, would the magic be broken, setting him free? He would see that she was only a pretty young woman.

But she squeezed her eyes shut more tightly, as if she were truly frightened of him. He felt that same fine shudder run through her body, conveying itself, like a warning, into his blood.

"Why?" he repeated softly. He wanted to kiss her closed eyes. He restrained himself. He had no business getting involved too deeply with this woman.

Why? Mitzi wondered, a small universe of emotions warring within her. Why? Why was she feeling this way? Why was this happening?

The owl, as if petulant at being ignored, continued to cry from the darkness of the hickory grove. It had its own question. "Who?" the owl demanded irritably. "Who? Who? Who?"

Mitzi tucked her chin down, so Mac's lips could not take hers again. She closed her eyes even harder, hoping the world would stop whirling so giddily.

No wonder owls were said to be wise, she thought desperately. This one was asking an extremely important question.

Who? Who was making her feel so bedazzled and warmly dreamy? And at the same time filling her with such alarm?

"Who?" the owl demanded again. "Who?"

The answer made her feel as if something inside her shattered and fell apart. She trembled again. For the answer was terrifying: *Who?* Not Barry. Not Barry, whom she had loved for seven years. Barry kissed her but not often and never like this. He craved attention more than physical affection. No, it was a stranger who held her, who had kissed her nearly insensible, who had made the stars spin so dismayingly.

His arms were still around her but motionless and taut, as if he sensed the wariness overwhelming her. She felt engulfed by shame. Her arms were actually around his neck. Her face was almost pressed against the width of his chest.

How could she do this to Barry, she wondered in disgust. How could she do it to herself? She had thrown seven years of devotion to the breeze and let this man kiss her. This man whose money probably assured him that he could buy anything. Anything and anyone.

The blood burned in her face. She willed her knees to stop shaking. Deliberately, with businesslike precision, she unlocked her hands from behind his neck and brought them down to press against his chest.

Firmly she pushed away from him, keeping her face averted. She felt as if her mind were willing a shield of ice to encase her body, to protect it.

At first he held her fast, but then his own body went coldly tense. He let her step out of his arms. He stood, watching her turn from him.

She moved away swiftly, until almost a dozen feet separated them. Then, far from his warmth, she felt secure enough to face him. Although she blushed, she knew the moonlight would not reveal it. She kept her face impassive.

"Well." She tossed her head slightly. "So that's what it's like to kiss—let's see, what are you?—oh, yes, a billionaire."

She shrugged again, looking up at the sky. The stars, it seemed, had returned to their proper places. "Interesting," she said, her voice almost clinical, "but nothing special. Well. It'll be something to tell my grandchildren."

She tossed him a deceptively calm glance. He stood, thumbs hooked on either side of his belt buckle, a shadowy figure under the stars.

She went on. "And you've satisfied your curiosity, I take it. So—can we go back?"

He didn't move. He shifted his weight so that he stood with one hip cocked slightly. The breeze played in his tousled hair. He regarded her carefully. She looked as cool as ice standing there against the starry sky. Her hair stirred around her shoulders, her skirt rippled against her thighs.

"That's why you let me kiss you?" he asked quietly. "Curiosity?"

"Yes." She nodded. The owl called again, and she looked off into the darkened trees.

"When you have those grandchildren," he asked, drawling the words out sarcastically, "who're they going to be calling Grandad? Anybody I know?"

The owl grumpily repeated its question: "Who?"

Mitzi clasped her hands together again in the billowing folds of her skirt. "You know who. You saw him. We've been in love forever."

Mac ran his fingers through his hair, pushing it back from his forehead. There was restrained impatience in the gesture. "No," he said.

She glanced at him sharply. She tried to calm her racing pulses. "No? What do you mean, *no*? We have. I've been in love with him since I was sixteen years old."

The wind rose slightly, and the trees rustled more loudly. A cricket began to sing.

"No," Mac repeated.

She couldn't make out his features, but she saw him shake his head stubbornly.

"You don't know anything about it," she said, just as stubbornly.

His voice was wry. "Maybe you thought you loved him when you were sixteen. You don't love him now. He's a habit you don't know how to break. And he doesn't love you. He's never loved anybody but himself."

Mitzi turned from him again, anger flooding her with hotness. He had no right to say such things. He didn't know what he was talking about. "Stick to counting your money. As a psychologist you don't have much promise."

"Don't I? As his fiancée, you don't show much promise, either. You kiss other men too damned well."

She whirled to level a hostile stare at him. "I don't," she informed him coldly, "kiss 'other men.'"

"Oh? You kissed me, angel. Like somebody who hasn't been kissed nearly enough. Somebody who needs it. A lot of it."

The observation stung, because she knew, to her shame, it probably seemed true. She blushed again and was grateful for the darkness. "I told you—I did it out of curiosity. And I didn't enjoy it nearly as much as you'd like to think."

"Could have fooled me."

Mitzi clenched her fists in frustration. She marched to the steps of the schoolhouse and began to gather up the remains of their moonlight picnic. "I've had a bad day. All because of you—and Polaris. It made me have trouble with my boyfriend—my fiancé—and I kissed you pretending that you were him, but it didn't work. You're certainly not the man he is. So now will you just kindly deflate your male ego and take me home? I'm tired of you."

Her hands full, she stalked to the Jeep. He followed her calmly, opened the door. She got in and concentrated on stuffing the refuse into the vehicle's waste container. He got in beside her.

"Yep," he said with elaborate casualness. "He's just a habit. You're a woman born to give. He's a man born to take. He caught you young, but you still have time to escape. I'd start running, if I were you. Maybe I just helped you take the first step. Someday you'll thank me."

She exhaled in impatience. "You don't understand anything about love. You don't understand real people at all. Maybe you shouldn't try."

He switched on the ignition and turned on the lights. He slanted her a coolly deliberate glance. "We don't seem to agree on anything. I think there's a moral here."

She returned his look as coolly as she could. "A moral? What?"

His mouth twisted sardonically. "One of us," he muttered, looking out into the gleam of the headlights, "has a *lot* to learn."

She swallowed and said nothing.

"Who?" demanded the querulous owl as they pulled away. "Who? *Who?*"

MILO'S SHERIFF'S DEPARTMENT car was parked in the motel lot. Although Mitzi protested, Mac insisted on walking her to the office.

When they entered, Judy's face looked harried. Milo, a big man of twenty-eight, with black hair and hazel eyes, sat behind the desk. He was on the phone, arguing with someone.

Mac frowned. "Is everything all right? Did our friend Tex stay quiet?"

Judy grimaced. "He's the *only* thing that's been quiet around here. Things got crazy. About half an hour after you left."

"Crazy?" Mitzi asked nervously. What was going wrong now?

Milo hung up, turned to say something, but the phone rang again.

"*That's* what's happening," Judy replied, giving the phone a look that should have melted it.

"Are you taking calls, MacLaren?" Milo asked.

Mac set his jaw. "No. My father's people have the number of my room phone. I don't need to talk to anyone else."

Milo picked up the phone, his face grim. "No," he said. "He isn't here. No. I don't know when. No, I'm not taking messages."

"What is this?" Mitzi looked in bewilderment at Milo, hunched grumpily over the phone.

Judy put her hands on her hips. She stared up at Mac in exasperation. "How do you *stand* it? How do you keep from going crazy? People—arrgh!"

"Sorry," Mac muttered. "I usually travel incognito. Word takes longer to get out. I apologize."

Milo, his brow dark with impatience, set down the phone only to have it ring again. He snatched up the receiver, his patience clearly at an end.

"What," Mitzi demanded again, "is going on? What's happened?"

Mac frowned in resignation. "I happened." He glanced at Judy. "Right?"

"Right," Judy answered. "And I bet I know how word got out—Sherry. Sherry's family has a gossip network where even the grapevines have grapevines. Half of Oklahoma's called."

"Called here? Because of—you?" Mitzi looked at Mac hopelessly.

Judy put on her glasses. She picked up a sheaf of notepad papers. "At first I tried to take messages. Then it got ridiculous. I made Milo take the calls. He growls better. He also sent away a reporter."

"A reporter?" Mitzi almost wailed.

"Our own dauntless Lyle Joe Dennis of the *Dancing Sky Herald*. Inviting himself to an exclusive interview. Milo uninvited him."

Milo hung up the phone.

"Listen, buddy, thanks," Mac said to him.

Milo started to reply, but the phone rang again. He answered it snappishly and once more began to argue.

"It's been like this all night," Judy sighed. She leafed through the notes. "First, a whole bunch of women, a lot of 'em teenagers, called up just wanting to talk to him. I was nearly giggled to death. Both the radio station and the newspaper from Talequah called up. Ditto Tulsa, plus the TV station."

Mac shook his head. He swore. "I didn't think anything'd happen this soon. Sorry."

"Listen," Judy said wryly, "it's been an experience. Five Realtors called, wanting to show you choice building sites. Four insurance salesmen called, wanting to insure whatever you build on your choice site once it's chosen. Six people called wanting to put in their job applications early. Four people wanted to borrow money, three wanted you to *give* them money, and five wanted to solicit money for their favorite charities. One wanted to know, quote, 'if your father's really as mean as they say,' and one would like you to finance the building of a commune devoted to the worship of quartz crystals."

Milo had hung up again. He looked disgusted with all mankind. He echoed Judy's question. "How do you *stand* this? How do you handle it?"

The phone rang again. Mac moved behind the counter, his face grim. "Like this." He bent down and with one neat yank unplugged the phone.

"That's what I've been wanting to do all night long," Milo said with satisfaction, leaning back in his chair.

Mitzi stared at Mac in horror. "You can't do that—what if there's an emergency?"

"Plug it back in," Mac said calmly.

She made a helpless gesture. "What if somebody has to call *here* for an emergency?"

Mac gave her a level look. "If it's a real emergency, they can have the police or sheriff's department get in touch with you."

She stared up at him, exasperated. "You mean I have to cut off my communications system? That's going to hurt my business—just because *you're* in town?"

He leaned against the counter, grinning at her exasperation. "I'll make it up to you," he promised. "Somehow."

His mocking smile made her perturbation flare into anger. He could never make things up to her. He had shaken her world to its foundations, pulled her contented existence down about her ears. If the whole of Oklahoma knew about him being here, then Barry knew, too. And probably he knew she'd been out with Mac. He'd think she'd betrayed him.

She felt sick inside. She'd never forgive Mac for doing all this. Never.

OUTSIDE, THE MORNING sunshine poured down and meadow larks sang in the pasture. But Mitzi, who had slept poorly, had a headache that surely had been intended for the ruler of a major country. It could not have been designed for an ordinary mortal such as herself.

She had tried to call Barry from her private phone last night. He hadn't answered. He probably wasn't speaking to her. She felt sick with guilt.

Mac MacLaren was apparently up and about his father's mischief. There was no sign of his dusty Jeep.

Tex Farleigh, the little cowboy, had arisen hungover and hostile. He stalked into the office, demanded his keys and muttered dire things about his constitutional rights being violated.

He paid her off with a check she was certain would bounce, and after he was gone, she discovered he had stolen all the towels from his room and, in a special fit of spite, the reading lamp, the bed spread and the toilet seat as well.

She thought of calling the sheriff's department, then decided she was happy simply that Tex Farleigh was gone for good, no matter how many of her worldly goods he had borne off.

She also decided she wasn't going to make up Mac MacLaren's room—she would not go near it. Sherry could take over that job. It would probably thrill her to death.

Mitzi made coffee and set out cups and complimentary cinnamon buns for her other guests. Then she plugged in the office phone and called Judy. "Listen," she said desperately, "you didn't say anything last night, and I was afraid to ask. Did Barry call?"

There was a moment of silence from Judy's end of the line. Mitzi sensed she was holding something back. "Yes. He called."

Mitzi winced. "What did he say?"

Another ominous pause followed. "He wanted to know where you were."

"Judy," Mitzi said desperately, "you didn't tell him, did you?"

"Of course not. I didn't mean to make trouble between you. But when I wouldn't tell him, he hung up on me."

Mitzi pushed back her hair and shook her head hopelessly. Barry's mood obviously hadn't improved.

"But," Judy went on, "he must have heard you were with MacLaren. He called again, right before you came back."

Mitzi's heart took a slow, unpleasant dive. "What did he say?"

"Milo talked to him. Barry told him he knew where you were. He said to tell you, 'Good work.' To keep it up. That he'd call you today."

"He said *what*?" Mitzi demanded, astounded. Although she should have been relieved, she felt hurt.

"You heard me. Don't ask me what's going through his mind." Judy's tone was clearly disapproving.

Mitzi sighed, thanked her and hung up. Immediately the phone rang. It was a reporter from Muskogee, demanding to be connected with Adam MacLaren, Jr.

Mitzi blithely said that no Adam MacLaren, Jr. was there, which happened to be true at the moment, then hung up and immediately dialed Barry's number at his ranch. He should not have left yet for the hardware store.

"Mitzi," Barry said sleepily. "I was going to call you later. I haven't had my coffee." He yawned.

Mitzi decided that she must brave the truth even if Barry was dangerously deprived of caffeine. She must tell him the facts before rumors went mad. "Adam MacLaren, Jr. is here. I went out with him last night."

He said nothing.

She swallowed guiltily. "I mean we just had a little to eat—"

"Yeah." Barry yawned again. "From Bubba's. I heard. What a tightwad."

"And we went up by the old Blackbird Hill School and talked. That's all."

Her cheeks burned, for she knew she wasn't telling the whole truth. More than talk had taken place between her and Mac. But his kissing had meant nothing, she told herself. It had meant so little that she shouldn't even mention it to Barry. Barry would only misunderstand and be hurt and angered.

"Mitzi, don't sound so guilty. I know you wouldn't do anything with him. If you did, you'd be a damned fool. A guy with his money isn't going to get involved with somebody like you. You're smart enough to know that. What did you find out? Anything that's going to help us?"

Mitzi took in her breath sharply. This was hardly the reaction she'd expected. Her emotions see-sawed wildly for what seemed the hundredth time in the course of twenty-four hours. "Find out? Help us?"

"What am I talking to, an echo?" he asked. "Lord, I need coffee. Yes. What did he *say*? Did you get any inside information we can use?"

Her stomach gave a sickly twist. She had imagined Barry in a dark rage of jealousy and pain. Instead all he felt was a self-interested curiosity. He didn't seem to mind in the least that she'd been with Mac. "Not really," she answered. "He said most of the merchants would be fine if they'd adjust. He said adjustment was the key.''

Barry was silent a long moment. Mitzi felt strange, as if someone had emptied out all her feelings, leaving her hollow. When Barry spoke at last, he didn't sound pleased. "That's all you found out? Look, did he say where he's going to put this store? That's important. You know I'm trying to get rid of this ranch. It could be a prime location for something like a Polaris store. Will you see him again? You could have put a bug in his ear about it. About my land.''

She ran her fingers uneasily through her hair. "I—I didn't think of asking anything like that. I was more worried about everyone in general—Tilly and Una, Lloyd Beecham . . . you, too. I wasn't trying to get inside information.''

"Well, honey, you ought to try," Barry said. "And don't worry so much about everybody in general. Worry about me, about us. How long is he staying?''

She swallowed hard. "He's registered for a week. Barry, I'm not sure I want him here for a week. He's—''

"He's got information that could be crucial to our future. Our situation is critical. I think it wouldn't hurt you to be nice to him. Cultivate him.''

"Barry! Do you know what you're asking? I'm not a spy. I don't *want* to be nice to him. He's . . . disturbing.''

Barry's tone became slightly patronizing. "Mitz, listen to me. This is a blessing in disguise. The guy's alone in Dancing Sky. He's probably bored. He's looking for a little action with the local ladies. You're right there, practically in his lap. He's here to exploit us, remember? Instead, *he* can be exploited. Just try to get any information you can get out of him."

"Do you know what you're asking me to do?" Her voice rose in indignation. "Don't you even *care* if I go out with this man—or what his intentions might be—"

"Mitzi, sweetheart, you know what his intentions are. Just don't give in. I trust you. I'm not asking you to do anything wrong—just be friendly. Make him want to do you a few favors. Treat him right—and we could be on top of a gold mine. I could be rich, and we could be married."

She clenched the receiver more tightly. She was having trouble thinking clearly. "Let me get this straight. You're encouraging me to play up to him. To go out with him if he asks. Pry information out of him. And see if he'd be interested in buying your land."

He gave an indulgent little laugh. "You make it sound so cynical, Mitz. It's just business. We'd be fools not to take advantage of it. Just keep me informed, that's all. Don't tell anybody else but me."

"You really don't care if I go out with him?" She tried to keep the disappointed tremor out of her voice.

"Mitzi, I know how you feel about me. Why should I be jealous?"

"Because," she retorted with hurt. "Because I've already told him I was in love with you. That we were going to be—that we'd been together for years."

"So *tell* him that I heard and was jealous. Fib a little. This is important, sweetheart. This is money. It's the future."

She said nothing. She gnawed unhappily at the corner of her lip.

"It's not just for me, honey—" his tone became soft and enticing "—it's for *us*. You can understand that, can't you?"

She didn't understand at all. Suddenly she felt more lonesome than she'd ever felt in her life. She mumbled something vague, said goodbye and put the receiver back in its cradle.

She stared numbly at her counter and the cash register. She went to the coffee machine and poured herself a cupful. She drank it black.

She looked out the window at the bright blue Oklahoma sky. The phone on the desk jangled shrilly. She didn't pick it up. She knew it would be someone asking for Mac.

She unplugged the phone so violently that she was shocked at her own childish show of temper. She poured another cup of coffee and sat down behind the counter, staring at nothing in particular, not allowing herself to think.

All she knew was that she was going to have to escape the motel. The office seemed to be closing in on her. She sat, allowing herself to feel nothing, waiting for Sherry to come so that she could flee.

When Sherry arrived, Mitzi spoke to her sharply about spreading the news of Mac's arrival. Mitzi, usually the soul of even-temperedness, nearly reduced her round little assistant to tears.

"And," Mitzi finished with a glare, "just so you'll know what you started, I'm plugging this phone back in. You answer every call. You tell them, 'No, Mr. MacLaren is not taking messages or visitors.' I want you to be firm. And so polite that it hurts. I mean it, Sherry."

Leaving Sherry wavering between a good cry and a bad sulk, Mitzi marched from the office. She got into her Toyota and headed without thinking toward Judy's, where she boarded her horse. She would get on Domino and ride until her head cleared and her chest stopped hurting.

Domino, an old black-and-white spotted gelding, was not handsome or swift. He had no pedigree, no particular training, and, if the truth were told, he was not especially bright. But Mitzi loved him with all her heart, had loved him from when she'd been given him, when she was twelve years old.

Domino was her companion when her thoughts were too deep or too complex for words. He was an ever-loyal friend who asked no questions, raised no doubts, passed no judgments. For years he had been her refuge in times of grief, worry, restlessness or even joy too intense to be spoken.

She parked next to Judy's stable. She saw Judy in the ring, on her horse Sequoyah, teaching the fundamentals of jumping to a little girl on a pony. Mitzi waved but didn't interrupt Judy or stop to talk.

She didn't even bother to saddle Domino. She fed him his expected carrot, then she curried him and put on his bit and bridle. She climbed up on a bale of hay and slid onto his broad back. His ears pricked up in anticipation.

Nudging his sides with her heels, she made a clucking noise. They set off at a trot, headed for the dirt road that ran beside the Sevenstar pastures, then she urged Domino to a slow canter. The wind tossed her hair and stung her cheeks pleasantly.

She rounded a curve and was surprised to see a gigantic black horse. It was a beautiful creature, standing fully saddled and tossing its head. By its fine configuration, thick mane and tail she knew immediately that the horse was an Arabian.

And just as immediately she recognized the rider, who was afoot. He bent over the horse's raised front leg, checking its hoof. It was Mac MacLaren, in blue jeans and a faded blue shirt, his gray Stetson hat pushed back on his hair.

He looked up at her with mild surprise, a slight frown crossing his face.

Coming upon him so unexpectedly brought all her confusion welling back. She didn't want to see him. She didn't want to talk to him, even have to look at him.

"Mitzi," he called as she approached. She didn't let her horse break stride.

Ignoring Mac, she kept her face straight ahead and nudged Domino harder so that he burst into his bone-rocking gallop. She streaked past Mac and the tall black horse, raising a cloud of gravel and brown dust.

"Mitzi!" he called after her again, anger in his voice. She refused to acknowledge him. She bent lower over Domino's neck, urging him to gallop even harder.

But even with the wind streaming past her ears and the pounding of Domino's big hooves, she heard an ominous sound, like low thunder behind her. It was growing louder.

Mac MacLaren had vaulted onto the Arabian. He was chasing her. And she had no hope of outrunning him. She knew it but leaned lower over Domino's neck, so his white mane fluttered in her face.

The hoofbeats grew relentlessly nearer, louder. The black horse loomed up next to her and her mount, appearing as if by magic. Domino, old and tiring, already had foam flying from his lips. Fear shot through Mitzi as she realized she was pushing her horse too hard.

She began to pull back on the reins, but Domino seemed to have so given his heart over to her wish to run that his momentum wouldn't let him stop. *No, Domino,* she thought, *don't try any harder!*

The big black horse kept pace with them effortlessly. A tanned and freckled hand shot out, trying to seize Domino's bridle. "Mitzi—slow down, will you?"

"I'm trying," she cried. She pulled on the reins, but Domino, confused and exhausted, was still straining to obey her original order.

For the first time the old horse failed her. He kept pounding on with all his strength until he stumbled. He pitched headlong in a fall, crumpling beneath her. He screamed with fright. She screamed in denial.

The ground flew up to meet her. She tried to fling herself away, so that the horse wouldn't pin her beneath his crushing weight.

CHAPTER SIX

"Mitzi!"

Mac had pulled his big horse up so short it reared, pawing the air. He leaped from its back. He was at Mitzi's side almost as soon as she hit the ground.

She knew how to fall, and she had landed, rolling, in a springy hummock of tall grass. The wind was knocked out of her, and she was badly shaken. Her knee was bruised, and her hands smarted, but she wasn't badly hurt. She was already struggling to her feet.

Mac reached for her, hauling her up roughly. "You idiot—why'd you gallop him? Are you all right?"

She stared up at him, angry but still disoriented from her tumble. She struggled to knock his hands away, but he held her fast.

"Get away—why'd you chase me? You nearly killed us. Let me go. I want to take care of my horse."

Her knees buckled slightly, but she caught herself. He gripped her arms more tightly. In his haste to get to her he'd lost his battered cowboy hat. The morning sunshine gleamed like fire in his wind-tossed hair. Concern mingled with disapproval on his face.

"Go *away*," she insisted, tossing her hair out of her eyes. She tried to shake herself free of him. He clenched his teeth in determination and kept her in his grip.

"Stop acting crazy," he ordered. "I want to know if you're all right, dammit."

She wiped her hand across one burning cheek, pushing aside an errant strand of hair. "I'm fine. Only my pride's hurt. Let me see to my horse."

He made a sound of exasperation and released her. "You'd better see to yourself, first."

Mitzi ignored him and made her way, staggering slightly, to where Domino stood, his eyes wild and his nostrils flaring. She thanked heaven he was back on his feet.

"There, there, big guy," she said shakily. She took his reins and began soothing him. She leaned her head against his warm neck and closed her eyes, trying to calm herself, as well. She inhaled his comforting scent of horsiness and hay.

She sensed Mac's presence behind her, felt his hands on her shoulders. "Are you all right?"

Suddenly she had an unaccountable desire to turn and lose herself in his arms, to lean on his strength and take shelter in it. *No,* she wanted to say, *I'm not all right.* She wanted to say that the whole town, her whole life, had turned upside down, and that the man she'd loved for seven years was acting as if all he cared about was money, and that she was angry and scared and humiliated.

But turning to Mac for comfort, when he had caused all the turmoil, was insane. She raised her head stubbornly. "I'm fine, no thanks to you," she said in a tight voice.

She bent and began to feel Domino's foreleg for injuries. Mac, sighing harshly, stepped to the horse's other side and ran his big hands down the other foreleg.

Satisfied that no serious damage was done, he moved an exploratory hand over the animal's haunch. Domino snorted restlessly and stamped, then finally yielded to the stranger's expert touch.

"You should know better than to run him," Mac grumbled, not bothering to look at her. "I wouldn't have come after you if I'd known you'd push this old nag—"

Mitzi shot him a glance of pure fire. "He's not an old nag. We can't all ride—" she looked at the big black mare "—Midnight the Wonder Horse."

He exhaled in exasperation. "All right. He's not a nag. But he's no colt. How old is he?" He gazed critically at Domino, an expression of slight distaste in his eyes. Compared to the sleek Arabian mare, Domino resembled an aged plow horse.

"Nobody knows how old he is." Mitzi's tone was dangerously clipped. "Over twenty. What's the matter? Don't you approve? Why don't you buy his youth back for him? You can buy everything, can't you?"

He took a step backward. His gaze, even more critical, fastened on her. "Whoa. If money could buy everything, I'd buy you a civil tongue."

"Buy yourself one," she retorted. She led Domino a few steps then swore under her breath. He was limping, although not badly. "Oh, *great*," she muttered sarcastically. "I suppose I'm lucky you didn't break his leg. And mine, too."

She began to hobble toward the edge of a grove of trees, Domino behind her. He favored his left foreleg slightly.

"Where do you think you're going?" Mac demanded, his voice almost a growl.

"To the creek. I want to let him stand in the water for a while. And to wash my hands." She looked down at her right palm. It was smeared with dirt and scraped slightly.

He muttered something he knew he shouldn't say in a lady's presence. He watched her limping away and resisted the impulse to kick something or break something or smash something. Her dark hair fell down her back in a rumpled spill, and the way she walked made her blue-jeaned hips sway in a disturbingly rhythmic way.

He set his jaw, leaned over, picked up his hat and put it on, pulling the brim down until it shadowed his eyes. He took his mare by the reins and set out behind the woman. It took him only a moment to catch up with her. She stuck her pretty little nose in the air, ignoring him royally.

"You know," he said, "if you'd stopped and just said a nice, neighborly *howdy* or something, this wouldn't have happened. Instead you zoom by me like a bat out of hell—"

"I didn't want to say a nice, neighborly *howdy*. I came out riding so I could be alone."

His freckled jaw looked as hard as granite. "You're not a mean woman. Not ordinarily. I don't think you have a truly mean bone in your body."

"Oh, really." She shook her head with impatience. "What would you know about the bones in my body?"

He pulled his hat down a fraction of an inch further. He gazed down at her until she felt the nape of her neck prickle. "Well, the bones of your body make a mighty nice framework, for one thing. And you're a sweet-natured thing. You've got fires, all right, but you keep them buried deep. Something's riled you plenty to make you act like this."

She looked at him irritably. Now he was making her feel childish and ill-tempered. It seemed that as soon as he'd exhausted one way of bedeviling her, he discovered another, more maddening one.

"Ah," he said with cynical satisfaction. "I know what it is. It's the jackass. Your boyfriend. He found out you were with me last night. It's driven him out of his head with jealousy. And you blame me."

She looked away, unable to meet his eyes. He didn't know how wrong he was. Barry would be dancing in delight if he knew that she was with Mac again.

"Why don't you go away before you make things worse?" The words were curt and she meant them.

He gave her a sidelong look. "I like you. I owe it to you to make things worse."

"What's *that* supposed to mean?" She darted another glance at him and was surprised at how grimly the muscles of his face were set.

He'd plucked a long-stemmed weed. He clamped it between his teeth. "I mean if I come between you and him, you should thank me. He's not much. You deserve better."

They had reached a grove of sweetgum and mimosa trees. She gave Mac an icy look and led Domino into the shade. Mac kept pace with her casually, as if they were out together for a friendly stroll.

"You don't know anything about him," she stated. "Barry's a very—sensitive person."

"Yeah. To himself. I could see."

"You're really being pushy, do you know that?" she asked.

He nodded calmly, unaffected by her barb.

They had reached the edge of Mongan Creek, a small, sparkling branch of the Rambling River. Wil-

lows joined the mimosa trees along the river's edge and
trailed lacy limbs in the water. The mimosas were in
bloom, their delicate pink flowers spangling the
branches. Their scent was so sweet it was almost intoxicating.

Mitzi led Domino into the shallow, tumbling waters
and let him stand, the cold current bathing his legs. Mac
gave his big black mare a pat on the hindquarters. She
stepped daintily into the creek beside Domino and began to nibble at a patch of watercress.

Sunlight filtered through the rustling leaves and fell
like bright coins on the water and the grass. Mitzi knelt
by the creek's edge and rinsed her scraped and throb-
bing hands.

Mac pushed his hat to the back of his head and stood
beside her, staring down. He made her deeply uneasy.

"So when did this guy—this Barry—claim you?
When you were in your cradle?"

She stood, still rubbing her stinging hand. She took
a step backward from him. "I was sixteen." She wished
he'd stop watching her so intently. "What difference
does it make?"

He didn't answer immediately. She turned, wiping her
hands on the thighs of her jeans. She sat down on an
outcropping of limestone, disturbed by his unrelenting
gaze.

He threw away the weed. He hooked his thumbs in
his front pockets. "I figured he got you early—when
you were young enough to be impressed by him. Then
he trained you. Now you're afraid to walk off and leave
him. You think he needs you."

She looked up at him sharply. "He does need me."
Yet now she was no longer even sure of that. It was one

more certainty that Mac MacLaren had shaken loose in her life.

"I don't think he needs anybody," he challenged.

She took a deep breath. She folded her hands together primly in her lap and stared at them. "You don't understand. He's very good-looking—"

"A problem I never had," he muttered wryly. She didn't look at him. He was a plain man, big and rugged and freckled, but she thought he looked fine.

"Barry's so handsome," she continued, taking another deep breath, "he's never known if people like him for himself. Or his looks. Or his money. His father had money."

"Well, now," Mac returned. "That could be a problem. Yes. I can relate to that. People might like him for his money. My heart bleeds."

Mitzi tried to ignore him. She plunged on. "His mother died when he was young. His father was very strict, and he paid more attention to making money than he did to Barry. When Barry rebelled, his father just packed him off to military school."

"The stuff of tragedy. You need violins to accompany this."

Mitzi, offended by his tone, lifted her chin defiantly. "Don't you *dare* make fun of him."

"Who's making fun? I empathize. It's my own story. I understand it perfectly."

She gave him a suspicious frown. "What do you mean? Are you saying that you—that your mother..." She left the question hanging.

"She died when I was six," he said matter-of-factly.

"Oh. I'm sorry." She felt embarrassed, as if she'd made a dreadful and painful mistake. But he seemed totally lacking in self-pity, and that bothered her even more.

"Well," she said with false brightness, "I'm sure you can also understand the part about his having a father devoted to making money."

"You could say that," he returned. He shook his head and leaned against the trunk of a sweetgum tree.

"I suppose you got sent to military school, too?" she asked, growing even more uncomfortable with his sardonic attitude.

He nodded. "All the bad rich kids do."

His easy acceptance made her feel more frustrated and embarrassed than ever. "Well, Barry went, and he straightened out. But it cost him. Emotionally, I mean."

He said nothing. He took off his hat and dropped it unceremoniously to the ground. He ran his fingers through his rumpled hair.

"Well?" she demanded, waiting for him to say something. "I suppose the same thing happened to you?"

He thrust his hand into his pocket. "No. But let's see. Speaking of cost—I owe you fourteen dollars, right? And nineteen cents. Do you want interest on it?"

"Of course not." She clamped her lips together in frustration and eyed him contemptuously. "And what do you mean—'no'? Military school didn't straighten you out?"

"No." He was counting out the money. "They kept kicking me out. All across the country. As my father said finally, I didn't seem born to conform."

"But—" Mitzi said, confused "—if you kept getting kicked out . . . how'd you ever finish school?"

"My dad finally sent me to a ranch in Texas for problem kids. Surprise—I liked it. I liked it better than prep school or military school. Or college, when it was time for that."

"You didn't go to college?"

"I dropped out. Went back to Texas. Drifted around for a while. Did what I wanted. Thumbed my nose at the world."

Mitzi stared at him, bewildered. "But what about your father?"

He gave her a slightly abashed grin. "He disowned me. Haven't you heard that rumor?"

Stunned, she nodded. Hadn't Tilly or Una said that Mac and his father didn't get along? "He disowned you? Is that what straightened you out?"

"Hell, no." He sounded truly surprised that she could think such a thing. "I didn't care about inheriting his stupid money. It made a prisoner of him. Turned him into a sour old man."

"You mean you just turned your back on everything?" she said in disbelief.

"I liked having my own way. And going my own way. He could keep the money."

He reached over and handed her the bills and coins he had counted out. His fingers brushed hers. Her hand seemed to burn at his touch. Hurriedly she stuffed the money into the front pocket of her jeans. "Well, something changed you. You're a company man now. Your father must have had something you wanted."

"He did . . . Power."

She looked at him questioningly. The breeze rustled his hair.

"I went my own way. The old man went his. We didn't always like each other, but finally we respected each other. He learned never to push me. And I learned what he'd really accomplished."

He stepped away from the sweetgum tree and stood in a patch of sunshine. "What he'd accomplished wasn't getting rich. That was incidental. What was important was that he'd built an empire that affected thousands of lives...that created thousands of jobs...that influenced the way life was lived all over the country—even in towns like this."

"In towns like this." Mitzi felt suddenly oppressed, as if by a huge weight. "Is that what gives you pleasure? Changing a place like this? Is that why you went slinking back and made it up with him?"

He raised one rusty brow and scrutinized her. "I don't slink." He stated it firmly enough to convince her never to bring up the possibility again. "I sent him a card one Christmas. That was all. I'd settled down by then. I'd done my helling, got it out of my system. I was foreman on a ranch down in Texas. Had enough money put away to make a down payment on a little place of my own. My father came to see me. But when he did, I'd grown up enough to understand what he was and what Polaris was. I didn't have to run anymore. I was ready."

"Ready for the money? And the power?" She couldn't keep the bitterness out of her voice.

"For the responsibility," he answered. "And everything that goes with it—good and bad. You've seen the bad. No privacy. Everybody wants to stick his hand in your pocket. That's what made my father such a bitter old cuss."

His eyes, gray as the Oklahoma sky in winter, stayed trained on her. Awareness of him tingled through her. He was an unassuming man, but his quiet force seemed threatening. She was filled with the desire to escape.

She stood up, spanking her jeans clean with a brisk motion. "How cozy for both of you. For you and your father. And how convenient that you finally saw the light. It mustn't be hard to miss, shining from all those heaps of gold."

He took a step toward her. "I told you. The money doesn't matter."

Her heart started to run away, a laboring, heavy gallop like Domino's. She kept a calm facade as she looked up at Mac.

"It's easy to say the money doesn't matter," she said, "when you're the one who's got it."

He took another step closer. She wanted to back away from him but refused to give him the satisfaction. He reached out and fingered a thick wave of dark hair that had fallen over her shoulder. He smoothed it, then pushed it back so that it spilled down her back. Her heart galloped harder.

"You know the problem with money." It was a statement, not a question. She looked up at him, fear and expectation in her eyes.

"The problem with money," he said quietly, "is it can't buy the things you want most. The things you want so badly that you ache. That's the problem with money."

A breeze came up and tossed the leaves more forcefully, making light and shadow play. The black mare raised her head and gave a low, delicate nicker. Somewhere a meadowlark burst into carol, then fell silent again.

"Now," he breathed, "kiss me."

His hands moved to her face, framing it. He tipped her head so that she had to look into his eyes and her lips were raised to his.

Slowly he lowered his head. In the dancing light of the mimosa grove, he kissed her until everything else was forgotten but the two of them.

CHAPTER SEVEN

THE MEADOWLARK called again. The breeze made the leaves of the trees rustle like silk, and the whole world seemed slightly drunk on the sweet scent of mimosa.

Mac's lips were warm and questing against her own, and his fingers were tangled in the dark wealth of her hair. Her arms circled his waist, shyly at first, then with a kind of desperation. He was doing it again, making the rest of the world insubstantial, forcing her to cling to him because he was the only thing that seemed solid or real or important.

His hands moved to her shoulders, then to her waist. He pulled her closer. Her lips parted in a small sob of pleasure, and he tasted her more deeply and sweetly still. His kisses burned with a slow, intense hunger that she seemed to feed.

The warmth of his hands through the plaid cotton of her shirt felt right to her. The hard muscularity of his back beneath her fingers felt right, too. So did the way his mouth kept mating with hers, as if too bewitched to do otherwise.

It all seemed so natural and good that she never thought to object when he lowered her gently to the ferny earth. The ferns were cool and yielding, smelling slightly spicy. He put one arm beneath her head as a cushion, and his large body hovered over hers as once again he ran his fingers through her hair, savoring its sleekness.

Ardently he kissed her lips, then her throat, then her lips again. He drew away slightly. He smiled down at her, touching her cheek. "You smell like hay and cinnamon and wind," he said.

He looked down into her eyes, his own growing serious. "And you taste like honey and wine. And you feel like—" he shook his head. "You feel like desire itself. You're a dangerous woman."

She was afraid to speak. She feared some spell would break.

He traced his finger across her lower lip, then her upper one. "I think we'd better talk. Before you get me into serious trouble."

He gave her a look that was part searching, part wry. Then he sighed harshly and lay on his back. He kept one arm around her and pulled her close, so that her head rested on his chest.

She could feel the strong beat of his heart. Her own was still running away crazily, like some caged thing set free.

"So talk to me," he said, lacing his fingers through hers. "Talk about anything. I'll hold you and we'll talk. That's all."

Again she was afraid to speak. She felt the rise and fall of his chest, and she looked with fond bewilderment at the tan and freckled hand that held her own.

His thumb caressed her inner wrist. "Tell me why they call this place Dancing Sky. Is it because of this?" He nodded up toward the lacelike leaves of the mimosas.

"Yes." Her voice was shy and soft as a whisper. "Because of the trees. If you're on the plains, the sky seems to go on forever. But here, because of all the leaves, when you look up, the light seems to be dancing."

"Nice," he said. He cradled her more comfortably against him. They both stared up at the spaces of blue sky flickering among the leaves. They were silent for a long moment.

Mac raised her hand to his lips and kissed it. "Maybe," he said, "we should be talking about *him*."

Him, Mitzi thought fatefully. Her runaway heart slowed, almost stopped. He meant Barry. Barry, whom she was supposed to love. Barry, with whom she'd been for seven years.

She went rigid with guilt.

He felt the tension invade her muscles, robbing her of her warmth and pliability. "Shh," he said. "It's all right."

But it wasn't all right and she knew it. She had been swept away by some intoxicating madness, but now its magic fled. Confusion seized her.

She'd betrayed Barry. She hadn't meant to, but it had happened. And yet, wasn't she doing exactly what Barry wanted? No. He hadn't meant this, that she give herself so willingly into the arms of the enemy.

She could not deny the power of what had happened between her and Mac. And she could not quite bear to move away from him yet. Somehow, paradoxically, he still seemed the only shelter her stormy mind could find.

"It's all right," he repeated, his cheek against her hair. "Tell me about him. How did he get hold of you when you were sixteen? You're too beautiful. You should have been taken even before then."

"I'm not beautiful," she said, feeling guiltier than before.

"You are. Why weren't you taken?"

She listened to the beat of his heart, compared its steadiness with the unevenness of her own. "I was one of those horse-crazy girls who never thought about makeup or clothes." She shook her head, wishing she could explain the whole thing to herself as well as him. "I had braces on my teeth and glasses. No boy had ever asked me out."

"And then this Barry saw what was hiding behind the braces and the glasses and the youth. And grabbed you."

Her smile faded. Barry—the shame came flooding back. She said nothing.

"And you thought you were lucky. Couldn't believe Mr. Wonderful wanted you, of all people."

Although no cloud moved in the sky, Mitzi suddenly felt as if the day had darkened and chilled. She made a small movement, trying to escape this forbidden embrace. The arm around her tightened.

"No," he said. "Tell me. Is that how it was?"

She bit her lip. "In a way. I thought I was the luckiest girl in Dancing Sky."

And she had believed it. Other people told her so all the time. Barry was handsome. He came from a good family, he had property, money, investments, everything. When things were going his way, he could be charming. What girl wouldn't have been dazzled?

"And you didn't mind that he was a weak, self-centered jackass?"

She tensed even more. Once more she started to draw away from him. But he only pulled her nearer.

"You didn't mind," he went on, "because you were the kind of girl who was meant to take care of things. You're the friend to all the stray cats and lost dogs and fallen birds of the world. You can even look at that old horse and think he's beautiful.''

This time she firmly pushed away from his restraining arm. She sat up, her face hot with embarrassment.

He stayed where he was, lying lazily on his back. He looked up at her through narrowed eyes. ''That's right, isn't it? You were the little girl who cried when the calves got roped at the rodeo. The one who bawled her head off when Bambi's mother got shot. And you couldn't help feeling sorry for a guy who was expert at feeling sorry for himself.''

She started to stand, to flee from this scene of humiliation. His hand snaked out and grasped her forearm, holding her momentary prisoner. ''I'm making a point.''

She looked away, glad that the fall of her hair hid her face from him.

''The point is this—I'm not saying you don't feel something for him. But it's not love. Pity isn't love. The urge to mother somebody isn't love. Whatever you feel for the guy, it *isn't* love.''

She still could not look at Mac. She thought of what Barry had said about this man—that he would never be interested in the likes of Mitzi, that he was bored and willing to trifle with the first local girl who came his way.

''You don't know anything about the way I feel,'' she protested.

''I don't think you know anything about the way you feel, either.'' There was an edge to his voice. He released her arm so suddenly that it sent a slight shock through her.

She stood up abruptly, brushing bits of fern from her jeans and plaid shirt. She pushed her hair back, trying in vain to smooth it.

He rose in one easy motion. Standing before her, he reached out and stroked her hair into place. "He won't like it that you're here with me," he said, looking down at her. "But I don't intend to leave you alone. I don't like him. I don't think he deserves you."

Mitzi's eyes stung with tears. Barry would be delighted that Mac intended to pursue her, whatever his motives. "You don't understand," she said. She shook her head helplessly and tried to blink back the tears. She didn't want to see Mac anymore. He made things within her feel as if they were tearing apart. She wished he'd never come to Dancing Sky.

"You just don't understand," she repeated, angry at him and herself and at Barry, too. Barry had put her in an impossible position. She stalked toward Domino, splashing ankle-deep into the creek, and took his reins. She led him out of the water and to the edge of the grove.

Mac stood, one hand on his hip, watching her go. He pushed back his unruly forelock. She wasn't limping now. She walked away with a perfect and deliberate gait, her back held straight. Her hips swayed with the determination of her stride. Her long hair swung down her back.

He set his jaw. She was leading that ridiculous plug of a horse and marching off like the queen of all creation. He had the impulse to follow her, humble her. He restrained himself.

He didn't want this woman for himself. She was delectable, pretty and honest and giving and unspoiled.

But not what he'd planned for himself. Not really. There were plenty of women back in California.

It was merely when he'd first seen her in the ice-cream parlor, working so earnestly to cheer up that sulky pretty boy Gabler, he'd wanted to save her from the jerk. And maybe have a little harmless fun while he did it. That was all.

He had no idea why every time they were together he ended up needing to have her in his arms. Or why the image of her blue eyes filling with tears bothered him. She'd cry more tears before it was over.

But it would be all right in the end, because he could help her save herself from that egregious jackass, Barry Gabler. Mac MacLaren was a man who understood power. He had the power to come between Mitzi and Barry if he chose, and he chose to do it.

She'd think her heart was broken for a while. There'd be more tears. But she'd get over it.

Of course she would. She was young.

THE MORNING'S EVENTS had humbled Mitzi so much that when she returned to the office she took no pleasure in Sherry's repentance. The phone was ringing madly when Mitzi strode into the office. Sherry ignored the jangling because she was nearly in tears, arguing with a man at the counter.

Mitzi recognized Lyle Joe Dennis of the *Dancing Sky Herald*.

"Mr. MacLaren isn't seeing anybody," Sherry insisted. "He's not doing interviews. I can't take messages for him."

"Come on, Sherry," Lyle Joe said in a wheedling tone of voice. "This could be a big break for me. The MacLarens hardly ever grant interviews—but he wants to cozy up to the people in Dancing Sky. That's what everybody says. He can't turn me away. He'll *want* to talk to me.''

Lyle Joe was a small middle-aged man with a protruding stomach, receding hair and an oily glisten to his skin. He turned his attention to Mitzi when she entered.

"What's the story, Mitz?" he demanded. "Give me the dirt. Come on. Do a pal a favor.''

She shook her head emphatically. "Sherry, answer the phone, then unplug it. The answer, Lyle Joe, is 'no comment.' As far as I'm concerned there might as well be no Mr. MacLaren here.''

"You can't deny he's here.'' Lyle Joe almost squealed in indignation.

"This is my place. I'll do what I like. Including asking you to leave, please. Right now.''

"I represent the press,'' Lyle fumed. "Why are you protecting MacLaren? Why? Is he romancing you? Does Barry know about this? Of course he knows. What's he think? Why isn't he doing something?''

Mitzi ignored him. "Sherry, go into my house. Put on some coffee for us. Unplug my phone, too. We're officially closed for business.''

"But—but" Sherry sputtered, bewildered.

"Closed," Mitzi repeated firmly. She switched on the outside sign that proclaimed No Vacancies. She locked the cash register. Then she turned and stared at the reporter in cool challenge.

"Don't try to treat me like this,'' Lyle Joe threatened, narrowing his little eyes. "I've known you since you were a skinny little squirt with a mouthful of metal. Watch it—or I'll see that your name and the name of this dump get spelled wrong in the paper for the next twenty years.''

"Well," Mitzi said sarcastically, "you've been practicing for the last twenty. You should have it down perfectly. Shoo, Lyle Joe. This place is closed. You're trespassing."

Lyle Joe opened his mouth to protest, but Mitzi took him by the elbow and led him to the door.

"They say MacLaren's considering buying Barry's land," he shot at her. "Are you cozying up to Mac-Laren? To make sure your boyfriend gets the lion's share of the goodies? Nobody in town'll appreciate *that*, Mitzi."

Oh, no, Mitzi thought, feeling worse than before. What if Mac really were interested in Barry's land? That would make her position truly dreadful. "Goodbye, Lyle Joe," she said firmly and almost pushed him out the door.

When he was gone, she indulged herself in a sigh, locked the door and went into her house.

"Is he gone?" Sherry's voice quavered from the kitchen.

"Yes. Thank heaven." Mitzi went into the kitchen and washed her hands. Sherry sat at the table, an untouched cup of coffee before her. She had her elbows on the table and her face buried in her hands.

"I'm sorry," she said miserably. "You were right. I never should have told anyone he was here. That poor MacLaren man. How does he stand it?"

Mitzi poured herself a cup of coffee and pulled up a chair across from Sherry. She patted the woman's shoulder.

"Don't worry how he's going to stand it," she said, sitting down. "Worry how *we're* going to stand it."

Sherry shook her head, still cradling it as if it ached. "Do you know how many people called? I lost count. People wanting interviews. People wanting money. Wanting jobs. Stock tips. Even *gifts*. It was a madhouse. What'll we do?"

"It's simple." Mitzi spoke with a conviction she didn't feel. "We just shut down until he's gone. We keep our phones off. Let MacLaren handle his own messages. And we don't let anybody else check in."

A horrible thought struck her. "Nobody else *has* checked in, have they?"

Sherry nodded even more miserably. "A reporter from Oklahoma City. And a woman from Talequah with three daughters."

Mitzi rationed herself another sigh. The reporter's presence didn't puzzle her, and she would simply refuse to let him stay a second night. The woman from Talequah—that mystified her, however. Talequah was so near, why would anyone come to Dancing Sky to stay at a motel?

Sherry must have read her thoughts. "Three daughters of marriageable age." She rubbed her temples gingerly. "They're all sitting around the swimming pool in their bikinis."

"The swimming pool? We haven't had water in the swimming pool for years," Mitzi protested. "As soon as I can afford to, I'm going to fill it in and make a rose bed."

"Well, until then, you have a bunch of women in bikinis lurking around it, waiting for Mr. MacLaren. How does he *stand* it?"

Appalled, Mitzi rose and went to the kitchen's south window, pushing back the curtain. Sure enough, artfully arranged around the empty swimming pool were three young blonde women, lying on beach towels, their bodies oiled and glistening. Although they were all large, their bulk didn't seem to bother them; they lolled as seductively as possible.

An older, heavier woman, obviously their mother, wore a gold lamé beach jacket and sat daintily in a lawn chair. She had large gold-rimmed sunglasses, numerous gold bracelets and read a copy of the *Wall Street Journal*.

"I think we've achieved true ridiculousness," Mitzi muttered bleakly. "They're here wanting to meet him, aren't they?"

Sherry nodded just as bleakly and took a stiff drink of coffee. "Are you really going to close down?"

Mitzi returned to the table. "We have no choice. We'll get the other guests out—" she nodded toward the direction of the pool "—then lie low."

Sherry looked both guilty and uneasy. "I don't have any right to say this, but I wish you'd stay open. I need the money. Both the kids' birthdays are coming up...."

Mitzi reached over and gave Sherry's hand a comradely pat. "You can keep working. There's always plenty to do around here."

Sherry brightened. She caught Mitzi's hand and squeezed it gratefully. "Thanks, Mitzi. Units three and four could use paint, and maybe we can have a general cleanup, fix-up week. Only..."

"Only what?"

"Only can you afford it?"

Mitzi managed a small smile. "Sure. We'll be famous after this—Mac MacLaren slept here. The motel of billionaires."

Sherry dug into the pocket of her smock. "By the way, not all of the calls were for him. Two were for you." She handed Mitzi two sheets of note paper.

Mitzi examined them with slight trepidation. Everything had gone wrong lately. She hoped the notes weren't invitations to even greater chaos.

The first was not. "Don't forget the business association meeting Monday night. Have heard you've talked with MacLaren himself. Good work—know you'll present the town's side clearly and fairly. Love, Una."

Dear, dependable Una, Mitzi thought with relief. She always kept her head. Una saw Mitzi's encounters with Mac as something that might work for public good, not private gain. Una was a pearl.

The second note gave her considerably less cheer. "Keep in touch. Remember everything I told you. Good luck. Love, Barry."

She felt cold all over when she read the message. She took a drink of coffee, but it didn't warm her. Barry still wanted her to act like Mata Hari or something—some sort of seductive spy. What he asked was so against her nature that she wondered if he really knew her at all, even after seven years.

A darker thought intruded. Perhaps, after seven years, she didn't know Barry. The idea filled her with something akin to terror.

"Mitzi," Sherry said with concern, "you don't look good. What's wrong?"

"Nothing." She stood, thrusting both notes into the pocket of her blouse. "Listen. Why don't you go home, change, then we could start working on those units this afternoon."

Sherry left and Mitzi went to the back window. She stared out the west window toward the pasture. Everything there looked peaceful, untouched and unspoiled. Whenever she needed strength, she turned to nature, and she badly needed strength now. Her trust in Barry was shaken. Her trust in her own judgment was just as shaken. And it was Mac MacLaren sowing these sickening seeds of doubt.

After a long moment she turned, went to the living room, plugged the phone back into its jack and dialed.

"Where were you?" Barry asked genially. "Why was Sherry answering the phone?"

"I went riding." She kept her voice even, matter-of-fact. "I met Mac MacLaren."

"Oh. Right. I've heard he's got a really gaudy Arabian out at the Sevenstars'."

"She isn't gaudy."

"Did you talk to him? Did you say anything to him about my land?"

"We talked. The subject of your land didn't come up."

Barry sounded both disappointed and impatient with her. "Well, Mitzi, sweety, *make* it come up. That's your *assignment*, honey. I thought you understood that. Were you nice to him? Can you make sure you see him again?"

She felt cold as well as sick. Couldn't Barry understand that Mac MacLaren was a dangerous man? "I don't want to see him again," she said, her voice strained. "It's not right."

"Mitzi, what's the matter? Don't you care about us? Don't you care about me?"

She thought she heard a slight whine in his voice, and it set her nerves on edge. The pit of her stomach swayed a little more uneasily. She was surprised to hear herself asking a question that seemed completely irrelevant.

"Barry, when your father sent you off to military school, did you ever think of—well—of rebelling?"

"Rebel?" He gave a short bitter laugh. "Are you crazy? That's how I *got* there. You don't rebel at military school—it's too tough. I learned not to cross my father. That's exactly what he intended me to learn. Why?"

She wasn't sure, but suddenly it seemed important. "I just wanted to know. You and your father didn't get along. Did you ever think of going off on your own?"

"And start from nothing?" Barry sounded indignant. "I'm not crazy. Listen, I'd have lost a bundle if I hadn't straightened out. And I wasn't born to be poor, Mitzi. No way. That's one of the reasons I don't ever intend to have to live off that motel of yours. I want better. We want better."

Dully, reluctantly, she admitted the truth to herself. Barry had never stood up to his father, and he had never done a single successful thing on his own. When things didn't go his way, he always blamed his luck, never himself. Because she'd wanted to believe in him, she had blamed his luck, too. She had never admitted to herself that Barry might be spoiled and more than a little lazy. The realization stabbed her. Out of mindless loyalty, she had deliberately blinded herself to his flaws.

She chose her words carefully. "Do you really want me to be 'nice' to Mac MacLaren? Even if he gets too friendly? You don't mind, as long as it helps sell your land?"

"Honey, we've been through this. I'm not going to get jealous. Why are you so stubborn? Look, I've heard he might choose either my land or Harold Swanson's. You be sweet to him, nudge him into choosing mine."

There was a silence, which she didn't fill, then, "Don't you love me?"

I don't know any longer, Mitzi thought wildly, and the knowledge horrified her. She didn't know if she loved him. Or if he loved her. He shouldn't ask her to see this man.

But the habit of pleasing Barry died hard. "I'll keep seeing him," she said unhappily. "If that's what you want."

"That's my girl," Barry purred. "That's my good little Mitzi who makes me happy. I've got to hang up now. Somebody's coming into the store."

She hung up. She unplugged the phone again.

She kicked off her boots and lay down on the old rose-colored couch. She was starting to ache all over from her fall from Domino.

But she knew it wasn't the fall that made her hurt deep within. She curled up tightly, hugging herself against a coldness that wouldn't leave her bones. She squeezed her eyes shut tightly.

"I do love Barry," she whispered fiercely. "I've always loved him. And he loves me." She kept repeating it. Perhaps if she said it enough, it would be true, and nobody, not even Mac MacLaren could ever again make her doubt it.

CHAPTER EIGHT

IT WAS FRIDAY evening. Normally Barry would take Mitzi to Tulsa or Talequah for their one big date of the week. But this was no ordinary Friday. Mac had changed everything in Dancing Sky, down to the smallest details of existence.

Mitzi spent the afternoon painting motel rooms with Sherry, in hopes she could exhaust her nervous energy and fall asleep early. That was all she wanted, a deep and dreamless sleep. Oblivion.

Oblivion, however, played hard to get. Mitzi planned a dismal supper of peanut butter on toast and then a hot bath and bed. All she got was the peanut butter sandwich.

Just as she swept away the meager crumbs from her sandwich, the back doorbell rang. She looked out warily and saw Judy Sevenstar, her brown hair plaited into one long braid. She wore jeans, riding boots and a pale green blouse.

Relieved to see a friend Mitzi swung open the door.

"I'll just stop a minute," Judy said. "Are you all right? MacLaren said you fell."

Judy looked truly concerned. "I'm fine," Mitzi murmured. She led Judy into the living room, and by old habit, they sat down on opposite ends of the rose-colored sofa. They had spent many hours on this sofa as they grew up. They had talked about everything in

creation. But suddenly an awkwardness seemed to fall
between them.

"I checked Domino for you," Judy said. "He's only
bruised. But I'd let him rest a few days. The old boy
isn't as steady on his pins as he used to be."

Mitzi nodded glumly. Domino wasn't as sure-footed
as he once was. He was one more beloved thing that
seemed to be slipping away.

Judy traced a pattern on the arm of the sofa with her
forefinger. "If you need to get away from everything
and want to ride, feel free to take Pirate. Anytime.
Don't even ask. That's one of the things I wanted to tell
you."

Mitzi smiled. Pirate was Judy's sweetest-natured
horse, a little pinto with one brown eye patch.
"Thanks."

Judy kept tracing the unseen pattern. "The other
thing I wanted to tell you is that rumors are going
around like crazy. You probably know."

Mitzi nodded.

"This is hard to say, but I thought you should
know." Judy met her eyes. "Some people are talking
against you. They say either that you're kicking Barry
when he's down or that Barry's using you like a puppet. But I tell them I know you. I don't think you'd do
either of those things. This whole thing may get pretty
crazy before it's over. But I'm your friend today, and
I'll be your friend tomorrow and I hope forever."

Mitzi gave her a shaky smile. "You're only terrific,
you know. The kind of friend I'd want forever."

Judy's slender face looked solemn. "I blame myself
for some of this. I pushed you into going out with
MacLaren. So if people are talking, it's because of me.
You wouldn't have gone if I hadn't been there."

"The talk will die down. It always does." But deep in Mitzi's heart she was unsure. Small towns had long memories. Scandals lived to a ripe old age.

After Judy left, Mitzi went to her bedroom and started to unbutton her blouse. She wanted a long warm bath and then to sleep so deeply that she forgot all conflicts.

But the back doorbell buzzed again. Hurriedly she rebuttoned her blouse. If it was another reporter, she thought, he'd better run for his life.

But it was Una. She had a worried air. Mitzi unlocked the door and led her into the living room. Una sat down in the oak rocking chair and refused an offer of coffee.

"I don't want to bother you," Una said, playing nervously with the band of her wristwatch. "But this town is going insane. Some people are talking about just shutting down business—right now. Quitting already. At least Lloyd is. And Tilly, too. She's gotten terribly emotional about everything."

"Lloyd can't quit," Mitzi said, sitting on the arm of the sofa. "That drugstore's his life. And Tilly can't either. That store *is* the two of you."

Una looked more uncomfortable than before. "I shouldn't even be here, bothering you. People are saying you'd probably be out with the MacLaren man—"

Mitzi lifted her hands in a gesture of helplessness.

Una nodded and kept plucking at her watch strap. "I wondered if he'd said anything to you. About how soon the store would be built. And where. And if this Polaris store is going to be different somehow—something that'll put us *all* out of business. Mitzi—terrible rumors are flying around."

"Una, please be calm," Mitzi begged. She was horrified to see the usually imperturbable Una distraught. "No—he hasn't said anything will be different here. And he said that we'd all be fine—people like you and Tilly and Lloyd—if we'd just adjust."

Una frowned. "I swear, my head's whirling so fast, I can't think straight. What does he mean—adjust? How do you adjust to losing the way you make your living?"

Mitzi paused. She wasn't sure, herself. For all she knew it was simply a neat answer, one the MacLarens had for everyone who objected to their ever-growing fleet of monster stores.

"Adjust—adjust," Una muttered. "How can we adjust when we can't even tell which end is up? People are already turning against one another. I've heard that MacLaren's already narrowed down the pieces of land he might want—Barry's and Arliss Crosby's. Barry and Arliss are at sixes and sevens now, and some people are quarreling about whether either should sell."

Mitzi frowned. "I heard it was Harold Swanson's land. Not Arliss Crosby's. Which is right?"

"That's what I mean," Una said with a helpless shrug. "Nobody knows. Some people have despair in their eyes—and others have dollar signs. Yesterday even Barry was ready to crawl into a hole and quit. Today he's practically dancing around. He doesn't even seem to mind that people are saying that's why you're seeing this—this MacLaren man."

Mitzi put her fingertips to her temples. Her head was starting to throb. *This MacLaren man,* she thought bitterly. *He's brought all this down on us.* "I'm not really *seeing* anyone. Except Barry. Nothing's changed." *Everything's changed,* she thought in despair.

"Well, why aren't the two of you out tonight?" Una questioned. "You always go out on Friday nights. Predictable as clockwork. This whole business hasn't come between you, has it?"

"No," Mitzi insisted, knowing she wasn't being honest.

"The business association meets Monday night," Una muttered. "I'd hoped we'd all pull together. Now I don't know. Everybody's half crazy. Tilly's simply spinning. She's even hurt that you're supposed to have seen him—the MacLaren man. She thinks you're striking out at Barry. Because he's behaved so badly lately."

Mitzi stared helplessly at the older woman. "Una— you know I'd never deliberately do anything to hurt Barry."

"Well, I *know* that," Una almost wailed, "but everything's become so odd. Mitzi, I hate telling you this, but I feel I must. Some people say you're throwing yourself at this MacLaren man because he has so much money. And others say you're seeing him because Barry wants you to. I don't know which story's the worse."

Mitzi set her jaw and took a deep breath. "I don't want anything from Mac MacLaren. No money, no favors, no inside information for myself. I've talked to him, that's true. I even thought maybe I could learn something that would help everybody. Not just me or Barry."

Una looked at her hopefully. "And?"

Una seemed so bewildered that Mitzi sighed. She rose and went to the rocking chair. She put her hand on Una's shoulder. "I told you. He said we should adjust. That's all."

Adjust, Mitzi thought hollowly. What a cryptic, meaningless word. It meant nothing to Una, who sat there worried and tired and confused. Mitzi had always thought of Una as unshakable, strong as the proverbial oak. Mac MacLaren had even her weakening dangerously.

"I shouldn't have bothered you. You're a dear young woman." Una patted her hand.

Mitzi smiled. Her smile felt mechanical. "It's all right."

But things weren't all right. And she wasn't a dear young woman. She was a desperate one. Although she smiled encouragingly at Una, she felt a heavy weight on her shoulders.

So this is what it means to be grown up, she thought unhappily. *When the people you always depended on start depending on you instead.*

Suddenly she was scared.

After Una left, Mitzi stripped off her work clothes and took a long, hot, stinging shower. She had wanted to lounge in a bathful of bubbles, but somehow the shower seemed more appropriate. She was starting to feel like a soldier in some undeclared war. And soldiers, she assumed, didn't soak in bubble baths.

She stepped out of the shower with her blood singing and her mind feeling so sharp it was almost frightening. She was going to have to go to the ranch and confront Barry. Things could go no further. What Barry was asking her to do was immoral. Mac, moreover, had told her outright that he wanted to ruin her relationship with Barry. If she didn't stop him, he would succeed. And Barry had to stop feeling sorry for himself and come up with a real plan for his life and his business.

She put on her long white robe with the little blue flowers and her matching blue slippers. Turning on the blow dryer, she brushed her hair until it shone.

She laid out fresh clothes on her bed: white lingerie, navy blue slacks, a matching blue and white knit top. She riffled through her small jewelry box for her white earrings and bracelet.

The back doorbell rang again just as she found her second earring. She hoped it wasn't a reporter, a sensation seeker or someone wanting a chunk of the MacLaren billions. She wished with all her heart that it would be Barry, come to his senses at last. She was so confused over Barry, she felt a smothering sensation in her chest strong enough to almost choke her.

She peeked out the window. Her hopes sank like a stone in water. Mac MacLaren stood in the moonlight. He hit the buzzer again.

One part of her wanted to ignore him, turn her back. But a bolder part was ready to face him, to square off with him for once and for all.

She swung open the door. "What do you want?" she demanded.

He looked down. Her robe was so white, it made her hair look jet black. He regarded the way her hair fell to the pale shoulders of her robe, the way that her body curved under the cotton fabric. He scrutinized her with such frank appreciation that she immediately regretted her decision to open the door.

"I said what do you want?" she repeated, her heart starting its familiar panicky gallop.

He opened the screen door, letting himself in. He stood right next to her, closer than necessary. "Sanctuary," he said.

"What?" He seemed to loom over her.

"Sanctuary." He closed the oak door, then faced her again.

She took a step backward. She touched the lace at the throat of her robe, making sure her collar was pulled tightly shut. "Why?"

"Have you seen them? The women? I drove up earlier tonight and there they were, four overweight blondes in lawn chairs, sitting out in front. They're wearing shorts that are too tight and halters that are too small. They giggle. They jiggle. They're drinking martinis, and they've got blood lust in their eyes."

"Oh, for heaven's sake," sniffed Mitzi, walking into the living room. "You're a grown man. You can take care of yourself."

He followed her. Without invitation he sat down on the sofa. He seemed totally at ease in her house.

She remained standing. "I didn't ask you to sit."

"I didn't ask to be besieged by killer blondes. They bumped into me when I was trying to get in my room. They kept knocking on my door. They tapped on my window. They even slipped a note under my door asking me to come out for a drink. I think they bored a hole in the wall to spy on me."

Mitzi shot him a blue glare of disbelief. "A hole in your wall? You're paranoid."

He reached into the pocket of his shirt. He pulled out a long woodshaving. It was curled like a corkscrew. "There's a hole in my wall, Miss Eden," he said firmly. "And if the blondes didn't put it there, the reporter did. There's a reporter from Tulsa hounding me, too. He's introduced himself. Four times."

Mitzi stared at the wood shaving in consternation. It was fresh, smelling of pine. It was tipped with the dust of plaster and paint. For all she knew, things had gotten so crazy that someone had indeed bored a spy hole in Mac's wall.

"I'll put you in a different unit." Her voice was flat with weariness. "They'll be out of here tomorrow. We're officially closed down until you leave. You're creating too much distraction. Too much extra work."

He leaned back against a plumped-up sofa pillow. He surveyed the room with an approving gaze. Then he turned his attention back to Mitzi. "I'm sorry. I usually register under a different name. But I wanted everything in the open. Well. My father told me it could get pretty bad. I guess he knew what he was talking about."

"Pretty bad?" Mitzi retorted. "It's a circus. If Prince Charles had come to town, there would have been less fuss."

He shrugged. "He's got less money."

"That's conceited." Mitzi shot him an impatient glare.

"It's a fact. Let's face it."

"I *hate* what your money's doing."

"So does my father—at least the silliness and greed it brings out in people. I thought maybe it'd be different here. It isn't. Too bad."

Mitzi studied him warily. His Western-cut shirt was dark green and made his hair look more fiery than ever. He seemed perfectly comfortable lounging there, as if he were settling in for the evening. His long legs were crossed, his arms draped along the back of the sofa.

She sat down in the rocking chair, tapping her foot impatiently. "You knew that you could walk into a place, announce your name, then sit back to see the fireworks go off? Is that your idea of fun?"

"No."

"Then why'd you do it?" she asked in exasperation.

"I told you. I thought it might be different here. Or maybe I wanted to be sure, once and for all, about what I was doing."

"What you were doing? What do you mean?" She frowned, tapping her foot again.

He looked her over again, from her gleaming hair down to her impatiently moving foot. She looked beautiful in white, like a flower waiting to be picked. He even liked the way she frowned. The slightly crooked way she held her mouth woke a small fire within him. He appraised her through narrowed eyes.

"Stop looking at me like that," she ordered. "Explain what you mean."

"This is a very homey room." He patted a pillow with approval. "Mind if I stretch out?" He moved the pillow, then started to uncoil himself to lie down.

"Yes, I mind," she objected. "Don't do that. Get up. Stop."

He put his hands behind his head. He gazed up at the ceiling. He wiggled his booted feet, which hung over the other arm of the sofa. "This feels wonderful. I love an old couch that's broken in."

"It's too bad your tastes are so simple when your life's so complicated," she replied, crossing her arms.

"You've summed it up beautifully."

"What?" He was irritating and impossible; as unpredictable as an Oklahoma spring.

"That my tastes are simple and my life's complex." He yawned slightly. "That's why I came to Dancing Sky unannounced. I wanted to see if it was still possible to go someplace like a normal person."

She fiddled uneasily with the lace at her throat. She felt as restless as a nervous cat. "You're not a normal person. You're not an ordinary man."

"Normal enough. Ordinary enough. When it comes to likes and dislikes. Needs. Desires."

Mitzi didn't like the turn the conversation was taking. "Will you leave? I was getting ready to go out."

"I'll stay. I love this couch. This is the kind of couch that money can't buy. I bet you stretched out here many a time. Reading, thinking, dreaming. I can almost feel the imprint of your body. The way your curves fit into the cushions."

Mitzi blushed furiously. "If you don't leave—"

"If I don't leave, what? You'll throw me out? Sounds interesting. Come try."

She rose angrily. She crossed the room and stood right over him. She stared down at him, her eyes snapping. *"Move."*

He gazed at her through half-lowered lashes. He gave her the slightest smile. "I told you. I'm not letting you alone."

"Then I'm letting you alone," she informed him. "I'm going to see Barry. So stay here, and have fun staring at the walls. Because when I come home, I'm not coming back here. I'll just let myself into one of the units. No blondes are chasing me."

"No," he said. "But I am."

He reached up and took her wrist before she could step away. His lazy insolence infuriated her. With her free hand she reached out and snatched the sofa pillow from under his head. She raised it and tried to strike at him with it. "Get out, you—"

His other hand sprang up, disarming her. With almost the same movement he captured her other wrist.

"Pillow fights?" he asked. "Never challenge me to a pillow fight. I'm invincible. The terror of the military schools—remember?"

The pillow, fallen, rolled away. The smile faded from Mac's face as he lay with both her hands in his grasp. He looked up at her face, framed by the white lace and the dark hair. "Come here," he said, drawing her down to him.

"No." She resisted weakly, but all her willpower seemed to flee. She sank to her knees beside the couch. Her eyes were almost level with his. Their faces were only a few inches apart. She noticed how strong his cheekbones were under the tanned and freckled skin, how thick his russet brows were, how coolness and warmth mingled together in his troubling gaze.

He was mesmerizing her again, and she both loved and hated it. "I'm going to go see Barry," she repeated. But she couldn't stop looking into Mac Mac-Laren's eyes.

He took hold of both her wrists in his left hand. With his right he reached out and stroked her hair. "You'll have a tough time seeing him. He isn't around."

She was starting to feel warm and dizzy. His statement unsettled her even more. Her breath became slightly labored.

His narrowed a bit more in satisfaction. "He's gone. He's nowhere around. There's nobody to save you."

Her brain spun. He sounded supremely confident of himself. How could he know anything of Barry's whereabouts? "Where is he? What are you talking about?"

He smiled. "He's in my Jeep. We switched cars. He's leading four blondes and a reporter all over the country in a wild goose chase. As a favor. Because he wants to be in my good graces. My very good graces."

"What?" Mitzi cried. Her mouth dropped open, forming a perfect *O* of horror and disbelief.

He reached out and traced that velvety *O* with his forefinger. "I met him this afternoon. I talked to him about his land."

His land. Mitzi pressed her lips shut and drew back. Mac really was going to buy Barry's land. It was true.

Mac wasn't daunted. His finger trailed along her lower lip, exploring the way it curved when she held it so tightly in control. "I talked to several people about land. But Barry seemed particularly anxious to please me. So when I came back and found I had a blonde problem and a reporter problem, I called my good friend Barry. I'm experienced at switching cars and losing people. I'm excellent. And Barry was only too happy to help. Which was truly giving and selfless of him. Because it leaves you all to me. And only me. With nobody to interrupt us."

How could he lie there, she wondered, smiling so casually, looking so comfortable and at home? How could he keep looking at her with such amused possessiveness and keep touching her as if he had every right to do so? Did he think she was for sale? That the whole town was for sale?

"What's the matter?" he asked. "There's nothing to stop us, Mitzi. He's stepped out of our way. Willingly. I told him I was coming back here. He had to know I'd come to you. He didn't mind. He was only too eager to let me."

"That's not true," she breathed. But she had the terrifying conviction that it was true, that Barry would do almost anything Mac MacLaren asked him. Now

Barry was out chasing around, happily making a fool of himself—and her.

All because of the money. The unspeakable Mac-Laren money. Mac must think it was wonderfully funny. He must think they were all dolts and clowns, easily bought, easily sold.

"Barry's land," she said between her teeth. "Will you really buy it?"

"Probably not." He tried once more to draw her nearer, but she held back, every muscle tensed against him.

"Then whose?" she demanded. She wanted to know. If she knew, she could put at least part of this insane charade to an end. "Harold Swanson's? I've heard that rumor, too."

"Maybe. But again, probably not. Stop trying to play detective. Just be a woman. Come here. You need to be kissed."

His hand moved to her jaw, half framing her face. His touch seemed to burn and freeze her at the same time. "If it isn't Barry's land and it isn't Harold's, whose is it?" she persisted. "You shouldn't keep it secret. The longer you keep it secret, the worse it pulls this town apart. Is it Arliss Crosby's?"

"No, angel." He smiled at her confusion. "Probably not."

He was teasing her, and though his taunts were almost gentle, she sensed a true ruthlessness beneath them. "Then whose?" She clenched her jaw, trying to resist his touch. "Somebody else. Who? Tell. And stop driving wedges and enmities between everybody."

He kept the same smile. It didn't seem menacing, but it frightened her more than ever. "Do you really want to know?"

"Of course I want to know." She almost hissed the words. Once more she felt like a small cat, one stalked by a creature far more powerful.

"Then come closer," he ordered softly. "Bring your lips right next to mine. And if you really want to know, I'll tell you. Then you can set the town at ease. The truth will be out. So just come closer. Just a bit."

Rebelliously she stared into his eyes, which seemed both mocking and tender. "Only because I want the truth."

She let his hand guide her face closer to his, until her mouth was less than an inch from his. She could feel his breath, warm against her skin, stirring her hair ever so slightly. His eyes were so close that she had to drop her gaze from them, and she found it resting on his mouth, with its strange curve, half-sensual, half-kind.

"I'm only doing this because I want to know. I want some of this craziness to end. If it isn't Barry's land or Harold's or Arliss's, whose is it?"

"Kiss me," he commanded. "Then I'll tell you."

She felt a frisson of danger so pure it chilled her through. But she wanted to know. A kiss would mean nothing, she told herself. He was used to buying everything. She would buy something in return—information that everyone needed, to put a stop to all the bickering. All it would cost was one perfunctory kiss, without significance.

He took her face between his large hands and leaned toward her so that their lips met. The instant his warm mouth melded with her fearful one, she knew she had been wrong. There was nothing mechanical in the kiss. It was full of feeling, far too much and far too powerful. And it had a significance of some kind, for it seemed to stab her through with sensations she had never felt before.

He kissed her long, he kissed her deeply, he kissed her until once more she was sure that the ordinary order of the world was rushing off, leaving her. She was stranded in some strange, magic and hypnotic world controlled by Mac MacLaren.

But it was a dangerous world, and she did not understand its laws. He felt the uneasiness surging through her and drew back slightly. He looked at her with his maddening half smile. "One kiss. It earns you one answer. What do you want to know?"

Her breathing was ragged, her breasts rising and falling under the thin fabric of her robe. "Whose land are you going to buy?"

He kept his hands on either side of her face. He stared at her lips, which trembled. His smile grew more puzzling. "I thought you'd have figured that out by now," he mocked. "You're smart, Mitzi. The land I want is yours. This place."

She was so shocked that she didn't object when he bent his face and kissed her again. This time he didn't ask, and he promised nothing in return.

CHAPTER NINE

As MAC'S LIPS took hers, Mitzi felt almost faint. For a moment all she knew was the warmth of his mouth as it expertly explored hers.

Then his words tore into her consciousness. She sprang back from him. She rose to her feet so swiftly that it made her head swim harder. Her robe had come loose. Belting it firmly, she stepped backward until she was halfway across the room. She stood, the ends of her belt still clenched in her fists, staring at him in dismay.

"What?" She kept blinking fast, because she wasn't even sure she was seeing clearly any longer.

In one easy movement he was on his feet, facing her. He pushed a hand through his unruly red hair.

"You heard me. It's your land I want. This and the pasture behind it."

Tears sprang into her eyes. "This is my *home*. My grandfather built this place. You want to buy it and tear it *down*?"

Suddenly he didn't look quite so confident. Her tears surprised and disturbed him. "Old things pass. New ones come. That's progress. I'll give you a good price."

She was so frustrated that she hit her fist so hard on the top of the end table that the table shook. "I don't *want* a good price. I don't want to sell. My family built this up from nothing."

"Mitzi, calm down."

"No!" She tossed her head angrily. "I won't sell. And I hope Butch Frost won't sell you his pasture, either. I love that pasture. It's beautiful. I love to watch the sunset there. You'd put your horrible store there? I *hate* you. Really hate you."

"Oh, take it easy." Irritation etched his face. "Stop being so emotional. It's just a pasture, dammit."

"It's not just a pasture. It's a piece of nature. And with all the people around here to sell you property, why pick on me? I don't want your stupid rotten money."

He set his jaw as stubbornly as hers. "It's the location. It's perfect. The best spot in town for a store like Polaris."

"I don't *want* to sell." She spoke from between clenched teeth. "I don't and I won't."

A tear coursed down her cheek and she scrubbed it away, humiliated that he had made her cry.

He gritted his teeth. He took a step toward her. She tensed and glowered at him.

"Look, Mitzi." His voice was stern. "You'll want to sell. Because that's the only way you're going to get what you think is your heart's desire. Believe me."

She looked at him with anger and distrust. Another tear spilled over. Again she brushed it away furiously. "What do you mean? What's this—another new game?"

He took another step toward her but stopped when he saw how truly upset she was. "Do you really want to marry that idiot, Barry?"

"Yes!" She flung the word at him, no longer caring if it was true. "I do. And don't call him an idiot!"

The slant of his mouth turned into something resembling a sneer. "Then you'd better sell. Because that's the only way you'll get him. If suddenly you have a lot of money."

The blood drained from her face. "That's a despicable thing to say."

"It's true. Let's face it."

"Barry and I are none of your business. Get out of our lives."

"No. There are at least three good sites for Polaris in this town. Yours is best. His is all right. But if he gets a big wad of money, he's not going to marry you. He'll invest it first, to make certain he stays rich, but he'll lose it like he's lost everything else, and he'll be right back where he is now. And so will you. I told you. He's a guy who takes. And takes."

"That's not true. He would marry me. He would." But suddenly she was no longer sure. Mac had loosed another goblin of doubt in her mind. Fresh tears rose, glistening. She couldn't stop them.

"Mitzi, why didn't he marry you when he had money? And if you really love each other, why don't you marry even if he doesn't? I think deep down he's scared. He'd have to provide for two when he can't even provide for one. I've seen his ranch. It's mismanaged. I've seen his store. He's driving it into the ground. I heard about his oil stock. If he'd half a brain, he'd have seen what the market was doing. He would have sold, gotten out in time."

"He's had bad luck, that's all," Mitzi argued. She wanted to believe it. She wanted with all her heart to believe it.

But she no longer could.

Mac's lip curled. "He's vain. He's self-centered. He might look like a dream boy to a sixteen-year-old, but not to a grown woman. He's trained you to look up to him and cater to him. He's got no business sense, no guts, and he thinks the world owes him a living. He's a loser. But if you want him, I can give you the money. And you can buy him. If you had money, he could play with it—pretending he's a golden boy again—until he loses it. But he won't marry you if the only prospect the two of you have is this—'' Mac stretched out his arm to indicate the eccentric little house and the motel. "He thinks he's too good for it."

Although his words struck too close to what she feared was truth, she raised her head in defiance. "Not everything in this town is for sale. And not everybody. Not me. Not Barry."

"No. Not you. Barry, yes." His nod was ironic. "You want him? I'll write you the check."

"This is really vile," she said, her voice filled with contempt. "You come to this town and play God. What gives you the right?"

"I don't need the right," he answered. "I've got the power. So—are you ready? Shall I write the check?"

She crossed her arms and turned her back. "No. Buy Barry's land. He wants to sell. I don't. I'm not interested."

"Is that the message he wants you to deliver?" His mouth had become a bitter line.

Her back stiffened, her shoulders going rigid. She bit her lip, trying to think clearly.

"I thought so," he said between his teeth. "He's using you. He wants you to talk up his land. So he can restore his fallen fortunes. You're well-trained, Mitzi. Naive, but well-trained. You're saying exactly what he wants."

She kept her back to him, but she sensed he had moved closer to her. She felt his nearness, and it sent tremors of awareness through her. "Then don't buy it. Buy whoever's land you want." She kept her tone icy. "Buy Arliss Crosby's. He's getting too old to work an acreage. He's a nice man. He could use the money."

He put his hands on her upper arms. "And what about Barry?" His lips were close to her ear.

She tried not to flinch. She tried to ignore how his touch both confused and excited her. "Barry and I can take care of ourselves. The world doesn't revolve around you and your money."

"I never said it did. But you put me in a dilemma."

"Would you take your hands off me?"

"No. I like having them on you. You make me think I ought to carry you into that bedroom and make love to you until you forget Barry Gabler's name. Forget he ever existed."

He brushed her hair aside and bent, kissing the nape of her neck. "Stop," she said, her voice unsteady.

"I won't make love to you," he whispered against her neck. He kissed her again, making her shiver. "Because then I'd have to go off and leave you. And you're too sweet for that. You deserve better. Someday..." He paused and kissed her nape for a third time.

She felt herself starting to shake all over. Her knees weakened and she was almost grateful that his hands were on her, holding her so that she didn't sink to her knees.

His mouth moved against her ear. "Someday a man's going to come along who appreciates you. Deserves you. Who'll want you and cherish you. Wait for him."

Mitzi summoned all her willpower. She pushed his hands away. She stepped away from him, crossed her arms over her breasts, then turned to face him. "Stop meddling in my life. It's no concern of yours."

He shook his head. "I've made it my concern."

"Don't."

"Too late. You've got choices to make. That's the way it is."

"I don't know what you're talking about. I made my choice years ago."

He moved to the brick fireplace and leaned against the mantel. He studied the pictures arranged on it—Mitzi's parents, herself as a child, a portrait of Barry, a snapshot of Domino looking over a fence. He picked up the portrait of Barry, looked at it critically, then set it back down, facing the bricks.

He took up the one of her as a child. She was grinning happily and staring at the world through her glasses. He smiled slightly, then looked at her.

"I said you've got choices to make. Do you want to sell this place?"

She stared at him. He bewildered her. He seemed almost gentle, lounging against the fireplace, holding her childhood picture. But he had awakened so many warring emotions within her that she was no longer sure he was quite human.

"No," she managed to say. "I won't sell."

"What if I forced you? I could, you know." He set her picture back carefully in place. He regarded her calmly, without rancour.

She knew he was right. He could force her to sell. He was too powerful for her to fight for long. He could do anything he wanted, ultimately.

He glanced at her childhood photograph again. He smiled. "You were a charmer even back then."

She said nothing in reply.

He looked her up and down, his face almost somber. "If I want this land, Mitzi, I'll get it. No matter how much it costs. I can build another motel. I can drive you out of business. I can make you come crawling on your knees, begging me to buy."

"Yes." She spoke the words as if they were poisoned. "You could. Does that make you feel important? Does that give you satisfaction?"

"No. Having power isn't always pleasant."

"How sad. I pity you."

"No," he answered. "You don't. Which is why you don't know what to make of me. You're used to a man who demands pity." He glanced at the back of Barry's portrait, leaning against the bricks.

He straightened and strolled back toward the couch. "I think I'll sleep here tonight."

Her eyes flashed. "You will *not*."

"Afraid of scandal?"

"Yes," she said frankly. "I was seen with you last night. That alone nearly ruined my reputation. You're not staying here. If you try, I'll leave and go spend the night at Judy's."

"Suit yourself." He stretched out on the sofa again. "You can come back in the morning and give me your answer. Or you can stay here. You may want to wake me up in the middle of the night to tell me."

"Tell you *what*?"

"How much fun power is." He put his hands behind his head and crossed his feet at the ankles. He looked approximately a foot too long for the sofa but seemed comfortable in spite of it. "Turn out the light when you go, will you?"

"Turn it off yourself," she countered. "And stop talking in riddles. Explain what you mean, about how much fun power is."

"Toss me that pillow, will you?" He nodded at the fallen sofa pillow on the throw rug.

She picked it up and threw it at him as hard as she could. He caught it expertly and stuffed it behind his head, then relaxed again.

"I really do hate you," she said. "Truly. With all my heart. I hope the ceiling falls in on you and kills you. I hope a copperhead slithers in and bites you."

"Someday you'll thank me." He yawned and covered his mouth. "Want to kiss me good-night?"

"No! Stop talking nonsense."

"It's not nonsense. I've got land to buy. I want yours. Barry's would do, but he's an SOB. I'd hate to give him the satisfaction. Arliss Crosby has a piece that'd do as well. You decide. Who gets rich quick?"

"Me decide?" Mitzi's eyes widened. She was horrified, appalled.

"You." He yawned again.

She marched to the sofa and stared down at him in fury. He returned her look with lazy insolence.

"You can't do that," she almost spat. She put her hands on her hips.

He quirked a brow. "Are we going to have another pillow fight?" He sounded hopeful. He also sounded extremely pleased with himself.

"No—and stop smirking. You're an arrogant lout."

"Exactly what my father used to say. No wonder this place feels like home."

"I'm *not* going to decide whose land you buy. I won't."

"You have to. I just delegated the authority. To you. Enjoy it."

"I won't accept the responsibility. *I* can't decide."

"I decided you have to decide. You can tell me tomorrow. If you haven't come back by morning, I'll meet you at noon at Judy's. In the grove. We can ride and talk."

He closed his eyes. Mitzi looked down at him with dread and anger. "Do you know what you are? You're a devil. A true devil. Red hair and all."

"Shh," he muttered. "The devil's sleepy. And you'd better go think. You've got big decisions to make."

She spun away from him and strode to her room. She slammed the door, threw off her robe and clambered hurriedly into her blue slacks and striped top. She thrust her feet into white sandals, then dragged her overnight case out of the closet, hastily packed it and snapped it shut.

Snatching up her purse, she opened the bedroom door and flicked off the light. Mac had turned off the living room light. She could see his long form, shadowy, stretched out on the couch. She stormed into the kitchen and slammed out of the back door, not even sure of where she was going. The door frame rattled.

She stood for a moment, breathing hard. She looked at the bright stars hanging over the pasture, smelled the sweet scent of rustling grass.

Inside the house Mac MacLaren stirred uncomfortably on the old rose-colored sofa. He had been able to imagine, all too clearly, what she had looked like behind the closed bedroom door, the white robe dropping from her young body.

His eyes had been closed, but in his mind he had been able to see how her blue eyes must have flashed when she left, how she would have tossed that mane of dark hair as she slammed the door behind her.

It had taken a great deal of effort not to go after her. What he'd told her was true—he should take her in his arms and make love to her until she'd forgotten there ever was a Barry Gabler. He should kiss her until she wouldn't say any man's name but his.

Restless he changed his position again, punched the pillow and kicked off his boots. Once more the memory of her tears bothered him. He'd have to steel himself. She'd cry over Barry Gabler, all right. But Mac had no desire to make her cry over him as well. When he finished his business here, he would have to be on his way, leaving her behind. That's how it had to be.

He frowned at the darkness. She'd told him he was playing God. She'd told him he was a devil. She'd told him he had no right to do what he was doing.

She was right. He was about to change this town forever. He was also shaking her safe, predictable little life down to its foundations, leaving it in ruin. He was doing it because he believed it needed to be done.

It was not a question of his right. It was a question, as he'd told her, of his power.

She'd understand soon enough.

MITZI DID NOT go far. She decided against involving Judy in this madness. She simply opened one of the motel units and spent the night there. The irony was not lost on her. Mac MacLaren had forced her into practically trading places with him.

He was comfortable in her snug little home. She was in a motel room, disoriented and perplexed. Until an hour ago she had resented how his choices could influence almost everyone in Dancing Sky. Now he was trying to force her to make the choice, herself, and take the terrible responsibility that went with it.

He was maneuvering her into an impossible situation, and so was Barry. Barry was playing right into MacLaren's hands, currying his favor, running his errands, acting the fool. And she knew precisely what Barry would tell her to do. He would instruct her to tell Mac to buy his land.

That wouldn't be fair or right. The thought made her more than slightly sick at her stomach. If she did as Barry would want, she'd be no better than a pawn. And Mac claimed that Barry would use her, then turn his back on her.

She sat on the bed in the darkness, staring at nothing. Barry had avoided actually proposing to her for years. She hadn't minded. She had stayed cheerfully faithful, waiting for him to get his affairs in order. But he never managed to do it. Perhaps Mac was right and deep down Barry feared the responsibility of marriage.

She lay down on the bed, her cheek against the pillow. The room was small, but the darkness around her seemed infinite.

She clenched her fist and gnawed nervously at her thumbnail, something she hadn't done for years. In the midst of all the puzzles and contradictions surrounding her, she was bewildered by the greatest puzzle of all—*Why did Mac MacLaren even care?*

Why should he care if she belonged to Barry? Had he taken that deep a dislike to Barry the first time he had seen him? And Barry, having displeased a MacLaren, must pay in blood.

Or was it something more primitive? Perhaps Mac wanted to drive Barry off, the way a range stallion would drive any other male from his territory. He felt compelled to prove his dominance.

But why? He toyed with Mitzi. But he didn't want her. He had told her as much. Someday, he said, another man would come along for her. She should be patient and wait for him. But, she wondered, could any man except Mac have such an impact on her? He had swept into her life like a comet. He had made her doubt a relationship she had labored at for seven years. He had changed the way she looked at everything, even herself.

She rolled onto her back and stared unseeing at the ceiling. She felt numb all over.

No man should have as much power as Mac MacLaren. It was impossible to fight him.

Very well, she thought, her fist still pressed to her mouth. She had only one choice. She would do the impossible. She would fight, anyway.

THE MEADOWLARKS sang to the morning.

Mitzi barely heard them as she got into her car. She was going to have to fight to restore sanity. She had heard that the best defence is a good offense. That meant she was going to have to confront Barry and not back down. And after that she would confront Mac as well.

The morning sun was bright when she parked her Toyota in front of Lloyd Beecham's drugstore. She walked past Tilly and Una's shop, heading purposefully for the hardware store.

The bell jingled when she opened the door. The inside of the store seemed unnaturally dark after the morning's dazzling light. It smelled dusty and somehow neglected. A fly buzzed at the front window.

Barry sat behind the counter, his feet up on his desk. He had dark circles under his eyes and hadn't shaved well. He was nursing a cup of coffee.

His blue eyes widened when he saw Mitzi. He looked around furtively, as if someone might be spying on them. He clambered to his feet as she approached.

She marched to the counter and slapped one hand on the brass cash register. She looked up at his chiseled features and perfectly waved hair.

He frowned, dark brows drawing together. "Mitzi—"

"I hear you were out being chased by blondes last night," she accused. "Shame on you. Shame!"

He drew back, surprised. "I didn't do anything wrong. They caught up with me in Talequah, made me stop and have a drink, that's all. The reporter, too. It was all like a game—"

She gave the cash register another angry smack. "If it's a game, then you're a pawn. What do you mean, doing Mac MacLaren's dirty work for him?"

Barry drew himself up to his full height. Haughtiness masked his features. "I didn't do anybody's dirty work. He asked for a favor."

"So he could come back and bother *me*. Don't you know he's making a fool of you, Barry? He's laughing at you. At all of us."

"Mitzi, hold your horses. It's a question of my land. We've got to be nice to him."

"Nice?" she tossed back in disgust. "The man camped out in my living room. He said perfectly dreadful things. He wouldn't go home. I had to leave."

Barry paled slightly. "Mitzi, you didn't make him mad—"

"Not madder than he made me—or than you did. I'm sick of this, Barry. We can't cater to this man. It's wrong, it's demeaning, it's—"

"It's life," Barry asserted, his face drawn. "And it's money."

"Oh!" Mitzi gave a huff of despair. "So it's all right if this man paws me and makes fun of you—"

"What do you mean, makes fun of me?" Barry demanded. "How could he make fun of me? I'm a person of consequence in this town."

"Not if you keep going off on wild-goose chases and letting Mac MacLaren *stalk* me like a—a—"

Barry's lip curled in disdain. "Mitzi, he's not stalking you, for God's sake. He's having a little fun. You don't have to fall into bed with him. All you have to do is keep him amused. Interested."

"I'm not interested in keeping him interested."

"Then," Barry shot back, his face flushing, "you don't have any interest in me. My future's at stake here. Our future. Did you manage to stop being offended long enough to ask him about my land?"

Mitzi felt her heart harden as if frozen. Up to that moment she had prayed Barry would act differently. She looked at him now as if seeing him clearly for the first time. His body was compact and perfectly proportioned. His hair gleamed blue black. He was so handsome he was pretty. But he did not seem to have an ounce of real concern for her or what she was trying to say.

"We talked about your land, all right." She felt dazed, as if she'd just awakened from a long, convincing dream.

"Well?" Barry leaned forward, his elbows on the counter.

"He doesn't really want to buy it."

There. She'd said it. Perhaps that would change things.

Barry swore. He straightened up. He kicked a wastebasket so that it toppled over with a clang. An empty cola can rolled out. He leaned back over the counter, staring into her eyes. "It's Arliss Crosby's land, isn't it? What the blue blazes does Arliss need money for? *He's* doing fine. He's got more than enough and he's an old man. Why should *he* get lucky?"

"It's not Arliss Crosby's land he wants. It'd be nice if it was. Arliss is a kind man. He's worked hard all his life. He deserves anything good that happens."

Barry rolled his eyes at the ceiling. "Spare the noble sentiments, Mitzi. Do you know what this means?"

"Of course," she answered with a calm she didn't feel. "You won't want to talk about getting married. But I'm used to that—"

"Married? Well, sure, there's that, too. But what am I going to do? If things don't shape up I'll be bankrupt. I won't have a dime. Whose land *does* he want? Harold Swanson's?"

Mitzi could feel the floor beneath her feet and the cash register beneath her hand, but nothing else seemed quite real.

"He doesn't want the Swanson land," she said quietly. "He wants mine."

The silence pulsed between them. Barry blinked once, hard. "Your land?"

"Yes. Mine. And the pasture behind my land."

Barry studied her for a long moment. "Honey, that's wonderful." He reached out and took her hand. "That's almost as good. Who owns that pasture? Butch

Frost? Does he know MacLaren wants it? Is there any chance we could get it first?"

"What?" Suddenly she didn't like the touch of his hand on hers. His fingers felt soft and damp.

He squeezed her hand. "We could get Frost's land before MacLaren has a chance. We could own the whole bundle. I'm mortgaged to the hilt, but you could get a loan on the motel. We could swing it—have MacLaren right where we want him."

She looked into his clear blue eyes. He suddenly looked more like the old Barry, the one who could be so charming. His gaze was affectionate, absorbed, almost happy. She'd always loved it when he looked happy. Now she didn't like it at all.

"I told him I wouldn't sell."

Barry's expression of affection vanished. He stared at her in disbelief. "You told him what?"

"That I wouldn't sell. And I won't. Do you know what he said? That you were scared to marry me. That you'd only do it if I had a lot of money."

Barry hardly seemed to hear her. He squeezed her hand so hard it hurt. "Mitzi, are you crazy? Sell to him. He'll pay you more than it's worth. I could invest it— get a fresh start—"

She wrenched her hand away. "No."

He came from behind the counter. He seized her by the shoulders. He peered into her eyes, his own pleading. "Listen. You've got to sell to him. Do you hear me?"

"No." Her voice was flat, without emotion.

"You've got to." He brought his face closer to hers.

"No."

"Did you tell him that?"

"Yes."

Barry chewed his lower lip. He glanced out the window. Then his eyes rested on Mitzi again. He gripped her shoulders harder. "If he can't buy yours, will he buy mine?"

"I don't know. Would you propose to me if he did?"

"Of course I'd marry you." He sounded childish and impatient. "But first I'd have to invest in something and make sure it was safe this time. That's only sensible. Now think, sweety. Did he give *any* indication whose land he'd want if he couldn't get yours?"

Mitzi stared at him, her eyes cold. "Which means more to you? Me or the money? If you had to choose, which would you choose?"

He sighed in exasperation. "Mitzi! Stop this stupid game and just tell me, will you? If he can't have your land, whose does he want, for God's sake? Did he give any hint?"

Mitzi felt a killing stab of disappointment in Barry, followed by a blaze of anger. *You don't really love me. Mac MacLaren's right.*

"He didn't say," she bit off.

Barry, she could see, was starting to realize how deeply offended she was, but he still couldn't make himself back off. "Mitzi, tell me everything he said. Anything. The information could be important."

She stared into his beautiful blue eyes. For the first time she realized a man didn't live behind them, only a self-centered overgrown child.

"He won't choose." She was careful to keep her voice even. "He told *me* to choose. *I* make the decision."

Barry looked at her dumbstruck. His jaw fell open. A disbelieving look crossed his face. "You're kidding. You're mad at me and you're kidding."

She pushed his hands away. "I'm not joking. Maybe he thinks it's funny. I don't. He said the decision's mine."

She took a step backward. Then she turned to go. Things had gone worse than she'd thought possible. She could no longer think straight.

Barry snatched at her arm. "If that's the truth, then I don't have to worry—right?"

He looked at her expression and amended himself. "I mean, *we* don't have to worry. Right? The two of us."

"I think the two of us may be past history." The calmness of her tone amazed her. "I'm going to have to think things over. Carefully."

She pulled away from him and nearly ran out the door. He ran after her. He caught up with her and grabbed her arm again when she was in front of Tilly and Una's shop.

"Listen—" he began.

"I wish you and everybody else would keep your blasted hands off me!" She jerked away. She started walking off once more, but again he captured her arm and pulled her back.

"Barry!"

"What's wrong with you?"

"Everything." She stared at him with disgust. "I just took off my rose-colored glasses."

She was furious, and she knew it showed. Barry looked suddenly desperate. Passersby glanced at them curiously. She saw Tilly peeping out the door of the shop.

"Mitzi," Barry said, trying to take her into his arms. "I *love* you. I've always loved you. Listen to me. We've got to talk...."

"We did talk. Let go. You're making a scene."

He raised his voice. "I said I love you. I'll say it in front of the whole town if you want. You belong to me. You have since you were sixteen years old. I love you! And you love me—you always have."

She stopped struggling. She gazed at him with a look that he'd never seen before.

"I don't think you love me. I don't think you've ever loved anybody but yourself—*Mister* Gabler."

She said it loudly enough for other people to hear. She shook her arm free from his grasp and strode away. She left him standing in the middle of the sidewalk, his face dark with anger.

She kept walking, her head held high. Her face burned with her own foolishness—she had spent seven years in delusion. Her future opened anew before her, and all she saw in it was emptiness.

CHAPTER TEN

"CAN I BORROW Pirate?" Mitzi asked Judy. Judy was mucking out a stall.

"Sure," Judy eyed her friend with careful scrutiny. "But you're not dressed for riding. Do you want to borrow some jeans and boots?"

Mitzi looked down at her blue slacks and white high-heeled sandals. She should have gone back to the motel and changed. Instead she had driven to Blackbird Hill and the old school house where Mac had taken her that first night.

She'd spent most of the morning there, strolling aimlessly through the hickory trees or staring out from the clearing at the hills and the river.

She'd thought hard as she stood on the windswept heights. But she hadn't once thought about anything as inconsequential as clothing. Judy was right. She wasn't dressed for riding.

"It doesn't matter." She still felt numb. "I'll be fine."

Judy studied her friend's pale face. She knew something was badly wrong, but she didn't ask what. "Let me saddle him up for you," was all she said. "You don't want to go bareback in that outfit."

Mitzi nodded, preoccupied. She glanced around the stable. She didn't see Mac's big black mare. "The

MacLaren man—" she began, not knowing how to ask the question.

Judy buckled the bridle and patted Pirate's patched face. Never before had she seen Mitzi so shaken. She kept her reply amiable but businesslike. "He showed up about ten minutes ago. He went the same way you went yesterday." She nodded in the direction of the creek and the mimosa grove.

Mitzi stared out the stable door, trying to hide her tumultuous feelings. In the nearest pasture, Domino grazed. He looked old and raw-boned in the noon light. "Domino," she said to Judy, "does he seem okay?"

Judy settled the saddle on Pirate's back and fastened the girth. "I looked at him this morning. He'll be all right." She adjusted the length of the stirrups. "But, frankly, Mitzi, I think he's about ready to retire. He's hobbling around worse than he should from that small an injury. He's old. I wouldn't ride him fast again. I wouldn't ride him much at all. Lately he doesn't seem as sure-footed as he used to. And I'm not sure he sees as well as he should."

Mitzi watched the old horse, browsing so peacefully in the summer grass. On another day, she might have reacted strongly to what Judy said, trying to deny it. But deep down she knew Judy was right. Domino was old. If she rode him again as she had yesterday, she might permanently injure him. She wouldn't be able to ride him much longer. The time was nearing to put him out to pasture.

And then the day would finally come when she would have to bid him goodbye forever. He would be gone.

Judy waited for Mitzi to say something, anything. When she didn't speak, Judy shook her head worriedly. "Look. You're obviously upset about something. Maybe I shouldn't have said anything about Domino. I just thought . . .''

Mitzi turned. She gave Judy a weak smile. "You're right. I've known it was coming for a long time. I just didn't want to admit it."

Judy's dark eyes were solemn. She led Pirate to the stable door. "Are you all right?" she asked Mitzi.

Mitzi nodded and took the reins. She vaulted into the saddle, although her sandals felt unnatural in the stirrups. "I'm okay." She was trying to convince herself as much as Judy. She looked down at her friend. "Did that ever happen to you—you suddenly realize something bad is true, and that in your heart you've known it a long time. You just didn't want to admit it?"

"Yeah," Judy answered. "A couple of times. Like when we lost the little Appaloosa colt. I kept telling myself we'd save him. But I think I knew we couldn't. Not really."

Mitzi nodded. She couldn't bring herself to say any more. In the space of one short morning she had admitted two such painful truths. One was that Domino really had grown old and would not be with her forever. That hurt deeply, but it was inevitable. It was nature's way. It was part of a great cycle that brought joy as well as sorrow.

But the other truth was more painful, because it was unnatural and shameful. She had been wrong about Barry. She had purposely fooled herself for seven years, seeing him as she wished to see him, not as he was. Mac MacLaren had known the truth about him immediately. And he had forced her to see it, as well. She could forgive none of them—not Barry, not Mac, not herself. The hurt was too new, too raw, and too humiliating.

She kicked Pirate into an easy trot, and the compact little horse responded with his usual eagerness to please. Unhappily she compared the smoothness of his youthful gait to Domino's creaking, lunging one. She stopped by the pasture's edge, dismounted and spent a few moments scratching Domino's ears, stroking his neck. "I love you," she said and pressed her cheek against his bony face. He nuzzled her neck.

Then she remounted Pirate and trotted toward the creek. She slowed when she came to the edge of the grove. Suddenly she felt frightened and empty, as if her heart had permanently vacated her chest.

She knew Mac waited in the dancing shadows by the creek. She could not see him, but she could feel him there, as surely as she could feel the wind stirring her hair.

She dismounted. Leading Pirate, she made her way among the trees. She saw the big black horse, standing by the creek, alternately tossing its head and nibbling at the tender grass that grew along the bank.

"Welcome," drawled a deep voice.

Mitzi looked around with a start. She saw Mac. He was stretched out lazily on a broad flat stone next to the creek bed. It was speckled with pale green lichen, and he leaned against another boulder, taller and also flecked with green. He wore black snakeskin boots, faded blue jeans, a white shirt and a black Stetson hat pulled down over his eyes.

He raised two fingers to the brim in salute. "Should I tip my hat? Should I stand? Or would you consider mere politeness as hypocrisy?"

She stopped, staring down at him. There he lounged, the author of all her problems. He'd shaken her life to pieces, but he was as relaxed as a sunning cat.

"Yes, you should tip your hat. Yes, you should stand. And yes, it'd be hypocrisy. But from you, even false courtesy would be an improvement."

He whistled softly. "I do believe I struck a nerve." He arose and swept off his hat. He bowed in a parody of a bow. The shifting sunlight played on the dark red of his hair.

She tried to ignore him. As usual, he filled her with maddening nervousness. She tied Pirate's reins to the trunk of a small willow so that he could reach the water if he wanted.

Mac had settled back on his stone, the water rippling only a few inches from his side. "Pull up a rock and sit down," he invited. "If you're not too fancy to sit on a rock. I didn't expect you to be all gussied up. I hope you didn't wear that outfit with seduction on your mind. It might work. I'll fight your charms as best I can, though. I did swear to try to be honorable."

Mitzi looked down at her blue slacks and striped top in frustration. "This is *not* seductive."

He smiled. "Then it must be you. Now—do you want to sit or not? We've got important matters to discuss."

He had his hat on again, the brim pulled down even further than before. If she wanted to look him in the eye, she would have to sit by him. It made her so angry she ground her teeth.

"Don't think of this as sitting," she warned him, as she lowered herself next to him. "Think of it as my descending to your level."

"We've got business," he answered. "We might as well make it pleasant. Wine?"

She sat stiffly, her legs crossed. His question seemed absurd. But he reached into the sparkling water of the creek and withdrew a bottle of Rhine wine that had been cooling there.

He set it on the stone and then reached into a saddle bag resting in the ferns next to the stone. He drew out a corkscrew and two wineglasses wrapped in white paper. He unwrapped them and set them beside the bottle. He removed the cork and poured. He held a glass toward her.

"Is this supposed to impress me?" she asked, amazed at his audacity.

He nodded. "I hoped it would. Take it, will you? I'm doing the best I can to be thoughtful."

She took the glass but didn't taste the wine. She kept glaring at him, but he was impervious. She might as well have glowered at the stones of the creek.

"I hope you don't mind cheese and crackers," he added, digging into the saddle bag again. "I'm just your basic cheese and crackers sort of guy."

He produced a box of crackers and a Gouda cheese, bright in its waxy red covering. He set it on a piece of paper, opened the cracker box, then took out his pocket knife and sliced into the Gouda. "Help yourself." He set a piece of cheese on a cracker and popped it into his mouth.

"Very cute," Mitzi said in disgust. "All your paradoxes and contradictions rolled up in one phony gesture. The billionaire cowboy stretched out by the babbling brook, snarfing crackers and drinking expensive wine. *My*, but you're an interesting man."

"So go hungry," he answered, unphased. "But you're right—the wine's good. A sin to waste. Let's drink to your better temper."

He clinked his glass companionably against hers. He drank. "To your better manners," she retorted. She wasn't about to be outbluffed by this man again.

He crossed his long legs at the ankles. He sighed. "It's happened. Power's made you edgy. See? It isn't all fun."

She set down the glass on the stone. "Isn't it? You seem to be having a wonderful time."

He ate another cracker. "Well, it's easier for me. Since you have to decide whose land I buy. Did you choose?"

She wished he would push the hat back. She still couldn't see his eyes. Just the lower part of his face, looking deceptively good-natured under his freckles.

As if he read her mind, he pushed the hat back. His even gray gaze met her crackling blue one. "Well?"

A simple glance should not have shot through her with such force. But she didn't blink, didn't flinch, even though her pulses speeded up.

"I made a decision, all right," she said between her teeth.

"And?"

His question hung in the air a moment.

"I won't be pushed into this. You want everyone in town to dance when you say dance. I won't. You can't force me."

"Can't I?" His smile was friendly but his eyes were cool and challenging.

"No," she answered, squaring her jaw. "You can't. You want to put me in an impossible situation. I won't let you. Make your own decision. Do your own dirty work."

He set down his glass. He leaned toward her slightly. "It's not dirty work. It has to be done. I'm offering you your chance. You may never get another like it in your life. Don't be a fool. Take it.''

"I'd be a fool if I did.'' She felt the anger rising in her again.

"Wrong.'' He put a finger under her chin, tilting her face up toward his. His expression was as defiant as hers. "You said I was trying to call the tune. You've accused me of that from the first. Of playing with your fate. Here's your chance. Choose your own fate. Or are you too cowardly?''

"I'm not a coward. You twist everything. You always do.''

"What's so difficult, Mitzi?'' His voice was low, almost a purring growl. He bent closer still. "It's easy. Pick your destiny. Just say you'll sell me your place. You know what happens then. You lose a patch of ground, but you'll gain a husband. That idiot will be down on his knees begging to marry you. He's too good to run a motel. But he's not too good to run through another small fortune.''

She turned her face away, no longer able to look him in the eye. He refused to allow her to escape so easily. He gripped her chin more firmly and made her turn back again.

"No,'' she whispered fiercely. "I won't sell. I don't want to.''

"Then it's easy.'' His own voice was taut. "Tell me to buy Barry's land. You really think that self-serving pretty boy loves you? Do you finally want to know the truth? Give me the word. I won't make him a rich man again. But I'll make him a well-to-do one. Is that what you want? Say it.''

"No!'' The denial was swifter and stronger than she'd meant it to be.

He studied her intently.

Once again she felt as if he were stealing her breath away, making her own emotions smother her. "It wouldn't be right," she said. "It wouldn't be fair. He wants me to—but it isn't right. And I won't do that, either."

His expression changed subtly. His fingers at her jaw grew gentler. She thought he had moved a fraction of an inch closer. She was too rattled to be certain.

"You've seen the light, haven't you?" he asked at last. "You've seen him for what he is."

She felt defeated. He'd done exactly what he'd wished. He'd come between Barry and her. In a bewilderingly short time, he'd ruined a relationship she had worked seven years to preserve.

"Are you happy?" Her voice was bitter.

"No. I don't like seeing you hurt. But you'll get over it."

"You're so blasted sure of yourself," she said with ferocity. She'd thought she was empty of tears, but fresh ones rose. She brushed them away angrily.

"No," he muttered. He caught her hand. Then he brushed the tears away himself. "You'll be all right. I promise."

She could only stare at him, perturbed as always by his actions.

"You'll be fine. Because you don't love him. You never did. It was infatuation. It turned into a habit, because you're a giving person. But you knew. You were afraid to admit it. That's all."

"That's not true." She realized new tears must have appeared, because once more he was wiping them away.

"It is. Don't mourn him. Because you don't love him. It's a fact. Let's face it."

He bent slowly to her, his mouth taking hers. His hands moved to either side of her face. In the beginning his touch was so gentle that it surprised her more than anything he had ever done. It was so tender, so concerned that it never occurred to her to object. She felt as if he were healing all the broken pieces of her emotions, making her whole again.

She didn't love Barry. Perhaps Mac was right and she had never loved him. When Mac's lips covered her own, she felt sensations that were new and dazzling. Barry faded away, an unpleasant lesson that had to be learned once, and now should be forgotten.

Mac sensed her response, shy and uncertain as it was, and took her in his arms. His touch was no longer gentle, but increasingly urgent. He pulled her so tightly against him that she felt her breasts crush against his chest with a sensation that was part pain, part pleasure.

His lips moved from her face, to her throat where her pulse throbbed strongly. Then his mouth traveled lower, resting between the full swell of her breasts. She could feel the heat of his kisses through the cloth, and his hands moved under her top now, spanning the bare flesh of her waist.

He kissed the tip of one lightly clad breast, then the other. She felt yearning swell within her. He raised his lips to take hers again. His hands moved upward, framing her breasts, then covering them. His fingers tracing their softness beneath the lace.

Then he was touching her beneath the lace. A gasp, half-frightened, half-pleased escaped her. He took advantage of her parted lips to taste her more deeply.

She instinctively drew her body back, although her mouth remained locked with his, as if she were his enchanted prisoner. But she knew, shame flooding through her, that if he were trying to teach her a lesson, she was all too eager a student. And he was too advanced a teacher.

He understood. As he did so often, he seemed to know her thoughts. His hands moved once more to her waist. He let her pull back slightly but kept her close enough so that his lips still touched hers, not in a kiss, but in the closest thing to it.

"If you'd loved him," he said against her mouth, "that wouldn't have happened between us. Would it?"

She said nothing. She felt the nearness of his lips, his hands still on her bare skin, his touch fiercely restrained, making no further demands.

"Would it?" he repeated.

She turned her face away. Yet, paradoxically, she found she was resting her head against his shoulder. Her arms were around him, shyly, against her will, as if she had no choice in the matter. She had to hold on to him, because, as usual, he had sent the rest of the world spinning off until he was the only solid and dependable thing left.

She kept her eyes closed. She felt safe in his arms, but knew she wasn't. She was in greater danger than she'd ever known. "What do you want from me?" she asked helplessly.

He gave a rough sigh. He stroked her hair. "Nothing. I don't want anything."

She shook her head but kept it pressed against his shoulder. "Why have you done this to me?"

"Shh." He kissed her ear. "It's all right. I wanted to set you free. That's all. I told you once. Someday the right man will come along. Wait for him."

The words stung. She should have sprung away from him, but could not. She felt the coarse cloth of his shirt beneath her cheek, smelled his scent, which was like the warm wind in the summer grass.

"And what," she asked, her voice bitter, "will I say about you, when all this is over?"

"What you already told me you'd say." He stroked her hair again. He made her straighten up. He tilted her face up to his again. His expression was remarkably solemn. "Someday you'll tell your grandchildren that you had an innocent interlude with a big old red-headed guy. But then you found their granddaddy. And really fell in love."

There it was again, Mitzi thought, looking up at him in despair, the speech that basically said, *So long, it's been good to know you, thank you, ma'am, and good-bye.*

"And what will you say about me?" she asked, drawing away slightly. "That once there was a damsel in distress in Dancing Sky, Oklahoma? And you saved her?"

He toyed with a lock of her hair. "I probably won't say anything. I'll just remember you. And hope you're happy."

"Well," she said with false brightness. "You don't tell a girl a lot of sweet nothings, do you?"

"No. I don't."

She drew back further still. She reached out for the glass of wine. She raised it to her lips and took a long drink, because she needed courage, even false courage.

He had released her. He sat, leaning against the boulder, watching her. "You're right," she murmured. "The wine's excellent. And the interlude we've had has been—educational. I suppose I should be grateful. Strangely, I'm not."

"No," he responded. "I don't imagine."

He sounded as weary as she felt. She wondered why. He'd played all the winning cards. The game was his. It always had been.

She stood, awkwardly brushing at her clothing. She had been a fool to let him kiss her again. She was like a stray puppy to him. He took her affection as long as it amused him, then he turned away. He had no real need of her. Her place was not with him.

She should be grateful, she supposed, that he hadn't seriously tried to seduce her. He was a man who always got what he wanted. He hadn't wanted her badly enough.

"I meant what I said about not making your choice for you," she said, smoothing her hair and adjusting an earring. "You've made your point. Now choose your own land."

"I don't have to." He looked up at her as he sipped his wine. He still looked preternaturally serious. He watched her as she moved toward Pirate. "You did it already."

She had taken the horse's reins. Now she let them fall back, still tied to the willow. "What?"

He nodded. He crossed his legs again. "You chose. You won't sell. You won't advise me to buy Barry's land. There's only one alternative. Left by default. I buy Arliss Crosby's."

She clenched her fists. "I didn't say that. I never said that."

"That's what it comes down to. You wouldn't choose your land. Or Barry's. Crosby is the only one left. He'll love you for it. Though I don't suppose everyone will."

She shook her head so hard that her hair swung. "Oh, no. Oh, no. I told you. I won't play this game."

He pulled down his hat brim again so that she could no longer clearly see his eyes. "And I told you. The choice is made. You made it. If you want to change your mind, you can have until Monday night. Until right after the much-discussed meeting. But then it's final. Unless you say differently."

With trembling fingers she untied Pirate's reins. She couldn't believe she'd lain in this man's arms, wanted to cling to him for strength and support. He was a monster of egoism, glorying in his power to make people jump whatever way he wished.

"You can't do this." She shook her head in anger.

"I've already done it."

She leaped into the saddle. She stared down at him, still calmly lounging in the same spot. "What about everybody else in this town?" she demanded. "You never told me how you expect them to survive. What are we to you? Just toys? Playthings?"

He pushed his hat down a fraction of an inch. "I told you. They have to adjust. You're a bright girl. You'll figure it out."

"If I were bright," she said sarcastically. "I wouldn't be here. But I can figure one thing out. I don't want to see you again. You can keep your room at my motel— but if anybody bothers you I won't be responsible. Stay out of my house. And out of my way."

"Maybe." He leaned back against the rock as if he were going to take a nap.

"Not *maybe*," she flung at him. "Absolutely. I *mean* it."

And, because she meant it and he seemed determined to pay no attention, she kicked the startled Pirate to spring off at a canter. She guided him in a tight half circle so that he was headed on the run straight for Mac. The little horse had to leap across the man's reclining figure. Mac ducked in surprise.

"Hey!" he yelled. But the nimble Pirate had already cleared him and landed in the creek bed with a splash. He kept running and then disappeared between the trees, Mitzi clinging low against the horse's back.

Mac stared after her. He threw his hat down and swore. She'd jumped the damned horse right over him. He'd seen its heels flash right in his face, and the horse had knocked over the wine bottle. Was she crazy?

Then, in spite of himself, he smiled. She'd done a fool thing, but she'd needed to do it. Exactly what he'd wanted was happening...she was becoming her own woman.

He'd hadn't done a half-bad job with her, if he did say so himself. He'd made her realize what a worthless piece of work the pretty-faced boyfriend was. He'd made sure the Gabler fool wouldn't ruin her life. And he'd finally made her show some of that fire he'd sensed within her from the first.

He nodded. Someday the right man would come along, and he'd see her and appreciate her and make her his own.

His smile faded. Whoever the man was who would finally possess Mitzi Eden, it wouldn't be he. It couldn't. He had other plans. Another road to travel. Another life, forever separate. He'd known that from the start.

But he'd set her free. Exactly as he'd intended. He wondered why he didn't feel happier.

He stood, putting on his Stetson. Then he bent and picked up his wineglass, which was, miraculously, unspilled. He raised it toward the trees through which she'd disappeared. Restlessness filled him. He needed to be moving on soon, he thought, to leave Dancing Sky and the woman behind him.

"To freedom," he said, and drank.

Nothing answered him except the wind.

CHAPTER ELEVEN

MITZI KEPT HER PHONE unplugged that night. She drew the blinds and kept only one small light on. She turned the stereo up high, trying to shut out the outside world with a wall of sound.

She sat alone in the semidarkness, feeling intensely miserable and listening to Kenny Rogers sing about feeling intensely miserable. She needed quiet, she needed peace, she needed a chance to sort through her broken illusions and find what was left in her life that was true and workable.

Any hope of quiet or peace shattered at slightly past ten o'clock. Barry appeared at her back door, pounding imperiously. Madness, which had come to town on Mac MacLaren's heels, rose to its full power again. Barry, who never drank more than one beer or one glass of wine, seemed drunk and combative.

"Mitzi, let me in," he ordered loudly. "I'm the man, I'm in charge here, and I'm going to tell you what to do. Open up."

You may be the man, but you're not in charge, and you're not going to tell me what to do, Mitzi thought. She refused to answer him. She didn't open the door. She turned the stereo up. A song about lying men and lost love filled the room.

"Mitzi, I'm not going to let you humiliate me in front of the whole town," Barry yelled. "And you're not going to ruin my future. Open up."

She stayed silent. She lifted the edge of the kitchen curtain so that she could watch him undetected. She flinched when Barry actually drew back his foot and kicked the door. "If you don't open up, I'll knock this thing down," he threatened.

For the first time fear flickered through her. She'd never seen Barry like this. What if he really kicked in her door? What would she do then?

He kicked again, swearing. This time the door shivered and the hinges groaned. "Mitzi!" he roared, then hit the wood with both fists. "You're not going to make a fool of me! Do you hear me? You're not going to make a fool of me!"

Suddenly Mac materialized out of the darkness and started talking to him. Mitzi couldn't hear what he said, but Barry, at first belligerent, began to listen, then to act almost deferentially. Even drunk, he was as handsome as a young god.

Mac, talking with quiet intensity, had the usual hank of unruly hair hanging over his forehead. His features were rough, almost plain. He wasn't handsome, but Mitzi's heart did a long, slow cartwheel as she watched the big man speaking quietly to Barry.

She forced herself back to reality. She had been staring almost raptly at Mac. She'd been admiring the ease with which he'd defused Barry. She shook her head scornfully. There was nothing to admire about Mac. He had no power except his money. His money spoke to Barry. That was all.

Perversely she wished Barry would act man enough to stop paying such devoted attention to whatever Mac said. *Don't listen to him,* she wanted to scream. *He's manipulating you the way he manipulates everybody.* She was the only one he had the courage to shout at? She wanted Barry to stand up to Mac. Defy him.

Instead Barry let Mac put a companionable arm around his shoulder and lead him away. The devil, Mitzi thought, he's hypnotizing him. *Barry, you idiot.*

Slightly hypnotized herself, she went to the front window of the office to see how the scene ended. What sort of snake oil was Mac selling poor, greedy Barry? What would Barry end up agreeing to do this time?

To her surprise a deputy sheriff's car drove up. Milo Sevenstar got out and started talking seriously to both men.

Barry looked hangdog. Milo, his face sternly official, seemed to be lecturing Barry about drinking and driving. Mac, his arm still draped around Barry's neck as if the two were brothers, apparently volunteered to drive him home.

Mac got in the driver's seat of Barry's beloved luxury Lincoln car, and Barry, without a word of protest, climbed docilely into the passenger's side. Mac drove off, Milo following.

Mitzi blushed. First Barry had acted like a wild man, then, just as bad, he'd been led off like a fawning dog, eager to please. Worst, his antics had earned him a police escort. Mac must have called for Milo as soon as he realized that Barry was drunk and bent on confrontation. She burned with humiliation, both for Barry and herself.

Half an hour later, Milo's car was back. Mac climbed out and sauntered almost aimlessly toward Mitzi's back door. He knocked. "Are you all right?"

She turned down the stereo. She swung open the door, glaring at him. "I suppose you thought *that* was funny, too—making a fool of poor Barry when he's upset."

Mac made a sound of disgust. "Will you ever stop feeling sorry for that guy? He made a fool of himself."

"He doesn't usually drink. There was no need to call the police."

"I don't know what he usually does. I only know what he was doing then. I didn't like it."

Mitzi tossed her head. "If your fortune ever fails, you can always make a living as a bouncer. You have a way with hell-raisers. It must be because you were such a good one yourself."

He cocked his head at an impatient angle. "I've made a career of avoiding fights. Somebody always wants to fight. Because of my size. Or because of the money. I don't play that game."

"No. You play your own game. What did you say to Barry, anyway? How'd you twist the truth this time?"

"I didn't twist it. I told him kicking down doors was beneath his dignity."

"Dignity?" challenged Mitzi. "You haven't left him an ounce of dignity."

"He hasn't left himself any. I also told him I wouldn't buy anything from a man who let a woman push him around. That if you wouldn't mind him, he was better off without you."

"You what?" She almost shook with outrage. "If I wouldn't *mind* him? I'm not a child—or a dog—or a pony."

He nodded. "You know that. I know that. He doesn't. A point you should remember. Besides, Mitzi, he'll never cross me. Certainly not for you. Not as long as he thinks he has a prayer of getting any money from me.''

She sighed, exasperated and defeated. ''All right. You proved it—you can buy a man.''

''No, I can't,'' he corrected. ''Not a good one. Another point to remember. He shouldn't bother you again. You won't need me anymore. I'll say goodbye now. I'm moving on.''

She stared at him, stunned. *Leaving?*

The thought cut far more deeply than all of Barry's petty betrayals, all of his shallowness. Loss swept over her. ''Moving on?''

His mouth crooked almost bitterly. ''You've seen the light. You're free now. I'll leave you alone, too. I'll go to Tulsa. Until Monday night. After your meeting. Then you can give me your decision. Whose land to buy. After that, I'll stay around a few days. Sign papers. Tie up loose ends. Until then, goodbye. And don't take any wooden boyfriends.''

Too stunned to speak she watched him turn and walk off. He was leaving. Just like that. He had appeared in her life with the suddenness of a lightning bolt, shivered her ordinary existence into splinters. Now, just as abruptly, he was departing.

She would see him again Monday night. Perhaps, if she were lucky—or unlucky—she'd see him a few times after that. Then it would be over. His life would diverge from hers so sharply it would be as if he had never met her.

''Wait,'' she wanted to cry after him. ''Don't go. Not yet.''

But she couldn't. She should rejoice that he was leaving. But she didn't. A hole had been torn in her universe. When he walked away, she realized something essential was leaving her life. Whatever it was, only Mac could restore it and make things complete again.

She supposed, numbly, that she had fallen in love with him. She stared after him into the darkness. To love him was folly. She might as well yearn after the wind or the stars. She could love him for the rest of her life. It would make no difference. A man like Mac wouldn't love back. Maybe he was so different from other people that he wasn't capable of loving back.

She closed the door. She turned off the stereo, and the silence closed around her. She heard his Jeep when it pulled away. She swallowed hard. She might see him only one more time. Monday night. That was all that was left. One single night.

MITZI WAS DRESSED in her best summer dress, a white full-skirted one, sprigged with small blue flowers. She had her hair swept up and her makeup carefully applied. She didn't feel quite real. She felt like someone in a play or a film.

She sat on a folding chair in the conference room of the First National Bank of Dancing Sky, her hands clasped in front of her. She was the first one at the meeting. Outside, the evening shadows stretched. She had come early because she needed to compose herself.

After Mac had left Saturday night, she had tried to think clearly. There was nothing she could do about her shattered romance with Barry. Their relationship was dead, over. She could never respect him again. Mac was right.

Neither was there anything she could do about her feelings for Mac. He had warned her he didn't love her. He had told her he didn't want her. Repeatedly he'd said that she was destined for someone else. She didn't want anybody else. When she saw him tonight after the meeting, she hoped only that she could conduct herself with composure.

She would tell him she hadn't changed her mind. She still refused to decide whose land he would buy. She refused to sell hers. And to ask him to buy Barry's would be servile and wrong. If Mac took that to mean he should buy Arliss Crosby's land, that was Mac's affair.

She'd sat a long time in the darkened living room the night Mac left, forcing herself not to think about the man who had just walked out of her life, or about how wrong she had been about Barry. She made herself concentrate on Dancing Sky instead. Dancing Sky was the only thing she might be able to do something about. She might stay sane if she thought about the welfare of the town.

The first thing Sunday morning, she called Barry and told him they were through. He was sulky and insulting. He claimed she had fallen for MacLaren because he was rich, but that she was a fool. MacLaren could have any woman he wanted. What would he ever see in a small-town bumpkin like Mitzi? He told her she'd proved herself unworthy of him. She thought she was better than she was. He didn't want her anymore. He hung up on her.

That afternoon Judy, looking concerned, came to see her. Somehow word had leaked out that Mitzi was supposed to decide the location of the new Polaris store. Judy said Barry must have let the news slip at the bar when he'd been drinking. Mitzi told Judy not to worry, but within she was deeply worried. Her foreboding proved correct.

The rumor had ripped the town right through its middle. By nightfall she'd had enough calls to force her to unplug the phone again. Some people were angry. Others sensed Mitzi had the power to grant some special advantage and wanted to seize on it. A few, like Judy, believed that Mitzi was doing her best to stay neutral, without taking favors or bestowing them.

Her most disturbing encounter had been with Butch Frost, who owned the pasture behind the motel and ran the town's auto supply store as well. He appeared at the motel Sunday night, demanding to know if it was true that Mac MacLaren wanted to buy their land. Mitzi, trying to be honest, said yes, but that she didn't intend to sell. Butch had turned almost purple with rage. "If you won't sell, I *can't* sell," he'd stormed. "It isn't fair! I don't need that dad-ratted pasture—*money* is what I need."

He'd stalked off, vowing never to speak to her again. Mitzi was too numb to care.

Now, as she sat waiting for the meeting to begin, she knew that nothing remained for her to say to Mac, not really. But after thinking long and hard, she had something to say to Dancing Sky. Tonight she would try to say it as clearly and honestly as she could.

The door of the conference room opened. Una entered, followed by Tilly. Una looked uncomfortable, and Tilly, disapproving. Mitzi knew the split between her and Barry had caused disagreement between the sisters. The knowledge saddened her.

She kept her head high. The dress she wore tonight had been ordered especially for her by Una, whose sharp eye had spotted it among a salesman's samples. Tilly's patient hands had altered it. She and Tilly and

Una were all a part of Dancing Sky, no matter what differences divided them at the moment.

She muttered a shy hello. Una answered, eyes down, but Tilly blinked hard and looked away.

The appearance of Lloyd Beecham, the druggist, spared the three further embarrassment. The president and vice-president of the bank came almost on his heels, followed by the manager of the radio station. At last the room was full.

Barry appeared at the last minute, making a display of ignoring Mitzi and sitting as far from her as possible. She held her head higher still.

Una, who was president of the business association, took the podium. She wore a summer suit of powder gray that matched her hair. She cleared her throat. When her eyes rested on Mitzi a moment, her gaze saddened.

"We all know why we're here tonight," Una said. "A Polaris store's going to be built. It will change the lives of almost everyone in this room. We know when it will be built—next spring. We don't yet know where, but—"

"Ask Mitzi Eden," someone shouted rudely.

"Yeah, Mitzi—where's it going to be?" someone else taunted.

She squared her shoulders, straightened her back.

Una set her jaw. "Where it's going to be built doesn't alter the fact that it *will* be built," she stated with military firmness. "That's what we have to discuss."

"*Where* does make a difference, Una. There's no pretending it won't," said the first speaker.

Mitzi gritted her teeth, recognizing Butch Frost's voice. He was still furious about his pasture. "It's bad enough that we have MacLaren coming in, muscling us out of our own territory,'' Butch fumed. "What makes it downright intolerable is that Mitzi Eden cozied up to him, and now she gets to play God. It isn't fitting.''

A grumble of agreement ran through the room.

Una raised her voice, her face deadly stern. "Let's deal with fact, not rumor. The question is—''

"The question is since when does Mitzi get to decide things in this town?'' Butch Frost challenged. "And the question is *why*? Why? Because she smooched up to Mr. Bigbucks when he came to town—''

"Yes—'' interjected Mrs. Hester, who ran the bookstore. She was a tall, middle-aged woman with firm opinions. "I don't believe she would have done it if Barry Gabler hadn't put her up to it. It's not her fault. She's young and confused, and now Barry's made a mess and dumped us all into it—''

"He did not,'' Tilly objected. "Barry's been an innocent victim in all this—''

"I can defend myself,'' Barry interrupted harshly.

"I think Mitzi has every right to do whatever she wants,'' Arliss Crosby said righteously.

"Of course, *you'd* say that,'' Butch Frost snarled. "You're the one who's going to end up the big winner. MacLaren'll buy your land—just because this dizzy woman is having a lover's spat with Gabler—''

"My land's as good as anybody else's and better than most,'' Arliss Crosby shot back. "You're so jealous you can't see straight.''

"The day I'll be jealous of you is the day hell freezes over,'' Butch roared. "I'm enraged by the injustice, that's all. Since when does some little hussy get the right to meddle...''

Una took off one high-heeled gray shoe. She pounded it loudly against the podium. "Order!" she demanded. "Order! Can we stick to facts?"

Momentarily an uneasy silence reigned. Mitzi took advantage of it. Self-consciously she stood. She kept her hands clasped together in the folds of her skirt. "Some of this controversy seems to center on me. I'd like permission to speak."

"Explain yourself is what you mean," Butch Frost cried. "Make excuses. Fat chance."

Una darted him a glance of intense disgust. "If you interrupt again, Mr. Frost, I'll ask you to leave. I mean it." She looked at Mitzi, standing all alone in the front row. "Permission granted. Go ahead, Mitzi."

The room went eerily quiet. Mitzi went to the podium. Una stepped aside and stood at the edge of the front row. Mitzi gripped the edges of the podium and swallowed hard. She smoothed a piece of paper out before her.

"I want to make a statement." She swallowed again. "Through no wish of my own, I've become involved in the decision of the location of the Polaris store. I've repeatedly told Mr. Mac MacLaren I don't want to be involved. He says the choice is mine, but I refuse to make it. I refuse, that's final. Mr. MacLaren knows my position. What happens next is solely his decision."

Her heart rattled fearfully in her chest. She looked out at the small sea of faces. Butch Frost looked irate and disbelieving. Una looked thoughtful and Tilly nervous. Barry stared out the window as if he held himself far above any nonsense Mitzi might utter.

"Mr. MacLaren has to decide whose land will be bought. I don't have the right, the authority, or the expertise to make such a choice. Nor—"

Her voice quavered slightly and she paused a moment to regain control. She took a deep breath. "Nor do I wish my personal life to be involved with the destiny of this town. Mr. Gabler and I disagreed about certain issues involving the Polaris store. Our friendship hasn't survived the disagreement. I'm sorry. But our relationship is nobody's business but our own."

She looked up again. Barry was staring at her now, disdain on his face. She knew he thought she'd betrayed him. That he thought she was a frivolous little fool. He looked as if he despised her.

She cast a swift look around the room hoping to see Mac. He was not there. She felt his absence like a physical pain.

She licked her lips. "As a business person in this town, however, I have the right to discuss how the Polaris store will affect us. Clearly not every merchant will survive the competition."

"You've got that right, cookie," growled Butch Frost rudely. He caught Una's fierce look of warning and clamped his mouth shut.

Mitzi stared down at her speech nervously. At least most people were listening. That was something. If what she said helped even one person, it would be enough.

"We face a giant," she said. "Polaris is a huge corporation, sophisticated and organized. They can sell goods at lower prices. This is a fact. We can't change it."

She glanced up. All eyes were on her, even Barry's. Barry's were saying, *What are you talking about, you fool woman?*

Her mouth felt cottony dry. "Polaris will always sell some things more cheaply than we can. But we can compete on other levels."

She heard a derisive snort and recognized it as Barry's. He laughed aloud at her. She ignored him.

"We can compete in the quality of what we sell. If Polaris sells a tool that's cheap, but that breaks in a year, then a hardware store can compete. It can sell a tool that costs more, but lasts."

Barry gave another sarcastic laugh. "You don't know anything about this, Mitzi. Sit down, will you? Stop embarrassing yourself."

She colored but plunged on. "Polaris stores sell low-cost goods. But they don't always sell the best. We can offer quality. We can offer service. A customer in a Polaris store has to help himself. I think Tilly and Una can survive the competition if they don't try to compete with Polaris's prices. They should keep doing what they do well now—offer quality goods and quality service. If I buy a dress from them, I know it's good and will last. They're concerned with niceties that Polaris can't afford to bother with."

She glanced at Tilly, who didn't look completely convinced. Mitzi squared her shoulders. "We can compete by having high standards. We can run our businesses as professionally as possible and never forget the customer comes first. We can make downtown Dancing Sky the most pleasant and polished place in the county to shop. Polaris can draw the customers who want bargains. But the same people will come to us when they want the best merchandise and the best service and the items Polaris doesn't bother to sell."

"She's just saying what MacLaren told her," Barry scoffed. "He's using her like a puppet. Shut up, Mitzi.

You sound like a television commercial." His voice became high and feminine, mocking hers. "Quality. Service. Standards. Send it back to MacLaren—where you got it."

"Barry, act like a gentleman or leave," Una ordered.

Mitzi set her mouth in a line of tight self-control. She pushed the rest of her speech aside. "I don't speak for anybody but me. I'm no puppet. All Mac MacLaren said was that we had to adjust. At first I didn't understand. Now I think I do."

"You don't understand anything, Mitzi." He laughed again.

"Barry!" Una reprimanded.

"I've seen Polaris stores," Mitzi retorted. "I've been in them. I understand what they can do and what they can't."

"Ha!"

"Look at Lloyd." She pointed at the elderly druggist, who looked startled. "A Polaris store can sell a toothbrush more cheaply than he can. But will it keep its pharmacy open at nights? No. Or on Sundays? No. Can you call it on a holiday for an emergency prescription? No. Suppose you're too sick to go out for medicine? Will a Polaris store deliver it? No. Can you count on the staff to remember personal things? No. I remember when my father was sick. Lloyd would call up and say, 'Mitzi, hadn't you better renew his pills? You don't want him to run out now and be uncomfortable.' And he'd deliver them, so I wouldn't have to leave my father. Would a Polaris store do that? No."

"It's true," said Arliss Crosby loudly. "When old Doc Henshaw made a mistake in my wife's medicine, Lloyd noticed. He knew there was no way she should have a medication that strong. He called Doc back and told him it was wrong. The woman might have been sick as a dog if he hadn't.''

Once more Mitzi cast a furtive glance around the room, hoping to catch sight of Mac. He was nowhere to be seen.

"He always orders special soap and lotion for me," Mrs. Hester added. "He knows that anything perfumed makes me itch. A Polaris store wouldn't know and wouldn't care."

"That's what I mean." Mitzi moved forward on the podium, trying to convey her earnestness. "Butch, remember when your daughter got that earache over Christmas? Didn't Lloyd open the store and tell you what medicine was best until you could get her to a doctor?"

Butch nodded sourly. Lloyd, a modest man, seemed embarrassed.

"What I understand," Mitzi continued, "is that Polaris can sell some things more cheaply than Lloyd. But it can't replace Lloyd. Lloyd is irreplaceable. Because he cares about us. He may have to adapt to compete with them, but he can compete. We all can if we care about our customers. We can work at it. Or we can turn up our toes and die."

She stopped, but the faces kept staring at her. Her courage suddenly vanished. She had nothing more to say. She had done her best. Only silence greeted her.

Then Barry smirked. He started clapping, very slowly. There was a horrible mockery in the sound. Mitzi stiffened slightly. She felt the blood drain from her face.

Una uncrossed her arms. She tossed Barry a withering look. "You're actually right, Barry. She should be applauded. Thank you, Mitzi.'' She clapped her hands together emphatically.

Somebody in the audience joined her. Then someone else did. Shyly, Lloyd began to clap softly as well. ''Thank you, Mitzi, for the vote of confidence. I'll try to live up to it,'' he said, beaming.

Tilly sat very still. Then she nodded. Quietly she added her own patter of applause.

Tilly's forgiveness and approval touched Mitzi so deeply that she felt she might lose control. She didn't know what to do or say.

Una spoke for her. ''When people come to shop here, let's roll out the red carpet. Let's make them feel welcome.''

''You know,'' Lloyd said, ''we could organize more sales. Offer more special events. Make things more fun. Get the community more involved.''

''Exactly,'' said Una. ''Like the Pioneer Days Festival. Frankly, we've never done much with that. We've been lazy.''

''We've got a nice-looking square, but it still could be spruced up,'' Arliss Crosby said. ''A few people—'' he stared pointedly at Barry ''—have let their stores run down.''

Barry gave Arliss an acid glance, then leveled the same glare at Mitzi. She felt more unreal than ever. How could a man who'd once seemed to love her give her such a look?

''Excuse me,'' Mitzi muttered, paler than before. ''And thank you for listening to me.''

She hurried from the podium. She moved as quickly as she could for the door. She escaped from the room, and then from the bank building. She was having an intense attack of delayed stage fright. Her hands shook and her breathing was shallow. Her stomach hurt.

Blindly she headed toward the square, which was leafy and placid in the lamplight. Her heart hammered and her breathing was still short. She kept thinking, "I should have said...I could have done everything better...I wasn't good enough."

She was exhausted, filled with uncertainty. She sat down on one of the benches. She buried her face in her hands. She didn't cry because she was too confused and weary.

Behind her was the pedestal on which stood the statue of the pioneer woman. The figure stared confidently out at the world and seemed ready to stride fearlessly into the future, head high.

Mitzi sat bewildered, head low.

"You did fine, you know." The voice startled her. It was unfamiliar, raspy and thin. She looked up startled. A little gnomelike man stood in the shadows. "I heard you," he said. She thought he smiled kindly. "You were remarkable. I heard you probably would be."

She gulped, unsettled still more. The odd little man didn't seem threatening, but he had caught her by surprise. "How did you hear me? I didn't see you there."

"I slipped in quietly. I'm not a particularly noticable man." He offered her his hand. "My name's Spaulding. D. L. Spaulding. You're, of course, Miss Eden. Mr. MacLaren sent me. The younger Mr. MacLaren. I'm his personal secretary."

She sat up straighter, more shaken than before. "Where's Mac? He said he'd come."

"He won't be here." Spaulding's voice was gentle, sympathetic. "He sent me for your answer. He said you were to choose the site of the new store."

She stared at the flowers bobbing in the moonlight. She shook her head. "You were there, you heard my answer. I won't choose. The decision is his."

He looked at her kindly. He was bald, and his rather large head gleamed under the streetlights. "You know what happens if you refuse to decide? He'll take it you've designated that he buy Crosby's land. By default."

She sighed. He seemed a nice little man, but he was an emissary from the palace of the foe. "He can interpret it any way he wants. I won't be bullied."

The little man looked philosophical. "He figured you'd say that. Which means he'll buy Crosby's land. It may make you enemies in this town."

She shrugged. "Then I'll have enemies."

The gnomish Spaulding stood quietly for a long moment. "He won't be coming back at all," he said at last. "Mac won't. There's been an emergency. He asked me to send his apologies. I'm the one who'll have to take care of details the next two or three days. And make arrangements to transport his horse. He'd left it at the Sevenstar place, thinking he'd be back. He was called away quickly."

Stunned she fought back the urge to cry. She had counted on seeing Mac at least one more time. Just once more. "I hope it wasn't anything serious," she managed to say.

"Most serious, I'm afraid. It's his father. Adam, Sr. He's been growing frailer and frailer. To be frank, Miss Eden, he's dying. Mac will have to take over the empire. It will create great changes for him. He'll hardly be able to call his life his own. Polaris is a harsh mistress. She makes enormous demands on a man."

"I'm sure she does." She smiled sadly. Polaris had been what Mac loved best all along. Now it would belong to him, and he would belong to it. He would no longer be the carefree prince, wandering the kingdom, amusing himself from time to time with a commoner like her. He would be the ruler, isolated from the ordinary run of men. He would live in a palace of absolute power, and she supposed it would be lonely. But he wouldn't mind that. He was strong. He was used to standing alone.

"You know," she confessed to Spaulding, "I never really knew why he came. Just to look the town over? And the sites?"

"Partly." He sat down beside her. "Planners had been here, looking. There was disagreement about the site. He came to decide, himself. And to investigate. He's been concerned with something that never concerned his father. Precisely what you were talking about tonight. Healthy competition. He wants to encourage it, not crush it."

"That's all?" she asked, a bit sardonically.

"That and the horse. He'd just bought that horse in Northern Texas. He knew it might be the last such outing he'd have for some time. Dancing Sky was on the route home. He could mix business with pleasure. I suppose it'll be his last sojourn as anything resembling an ordinary citizen. As I said, everything will change for him now. I don't envy him, actually."

They sat in silence. He reached over and patted her hand. "Do you have any message for him? He's back in California, of course, with his father. But I'll be glad to take any word you send."

She stared down into her lap. Spaulding was right. Everything had changed, as Mac had always known it must. "No. Just that I'm sorry his father's ill. I know how it is."

"Well." Spaulding coughed self-consciously, then stood. He shook her hand again. "A pleasure to meet you, Miss Eden. I hope your townsmen take to heart what you said. Mr. MacLaren sends you his best wishes. And this."

He reached into the pocket of his suit coat and drew out an envelope. "Good night," he said. "I'll probably see you in passing. I'm registered at your unique little motel. Your assistant checked me in."

He clicked his heels together, turned and left so swiftly that it seemed he vanished by magic. She stared off into the shadows, puzzled. What an odd little man— like a messenger from another world.

She looked numbly at the envelope in her hand. Just as numbly, she opened it. The note was short.

Hey, Mitzi—
   Remember what I told you. You're special. Keep waiting. Your prince will come. Fond thoughts—
                                            Mac

She stood up, holding the paper carefully. That was all she had left. Four short sentences and a farewell. Their finality seemed to echo through the night.

She turned and looked up at the statue of the pioneer woman. Then she turned back, her hands deep in the pockets of her skirt. She wanted to walk, nowhere in particular, just to walk.

The big summer stars glittered overhead. She felt incredibly alone. He was gone for good now. It felt like a small death.

TWO DAYS LATER she heard that Adam MacLaren, Sr. had died in his sleep, a victim of lingering heart disease. His corporation passed smoothly and officially into the hands of his son. Mitzi tried to imagine Mac in a business suit and could not. She wrote him a note of sympathy and mailed it. She got no answer. She had expected none.

The Polaris corporation bought Arliss Crosby's land, Mr. Spaulding overseeing the legal details. Arliss was the happiest man in Dancing Sky.

Butch Frost deeply resented that Arliss's land, not his, had been bought. He refused to speak to Mitzi. Barry, too, had stopped speaking to her, but he began speaking against her. Looking for sympathy, he spread so many rumors, half truths and outright lies that in the end nobody believed him. Even the normally devoted Tilly told him to straighten up and act like a man.

Slowly most of the other rifts in Dancing Sky healed. Una, finding new reserves of energy, called extra meetings to rally the town's merchants against the challenge Polaris soon would offer.

Summer turned into autumn. Mitzi thought constantly of Mac. She tried to envision him as a tycoon working a sixteen-hour day, a phone in his limousine. She couldn't. Somehow she couldn't imagine him as a merchant king. To her he was Mac, big, rangy, redheaded and strong-willed. She missed everything about him, complex and contradictory as he was.

A cattle corporation from out of state bought Barry's ranch. He immediately shut down the hardware store, put a For Sale on it and moved to Tulsa. Mitzi heard he invested all his money in a restaurant. It took only a short time for rumors to reach Dancing Sky that the restaurant was doing poorly, steadily losing money.

Mitzi was sorry but didn't miss him. It was as if it was a different person, not her, who had been involved with Barry. It all seemed to have happened a lifetime ago.

Autumn drifted into the short, barren Oklahoma winter. Domino grew creakier and slower. He fell again, one winter morning when the cold air made him want to gallop. Mitzi wasn't hurt, but he was. She knew it was time to put him out to pasture for good. Judy sadly agreed.

Mitzi went to visit him, but everytime she saw him, she found herself thinking of Mac. Sometimes she just stood out in the field with the old horse, her arms around his neck, her face pressed against his coarse mane.

She remembered how Mac had held her in his arms after Domino fell the first time. She remembered him stretched out on her old sofa, taking her face between his hands and bending to kiss her. She remembered how he had kissed her beside the creek and how his mouth had tasted like wine and his arms had felt like a beloved home. She missed him so much she couldn't speak of it.

Judy had asked her tactfully if she wanted to talk about Mac and what had happened. Mitzi said no. She didn't know if she would ever be able to talk about it.

Spring came. Bulldozers scraped Arliss Crosby's land flat for the new Polaris store. Soon a great raw hole gaped in the earth. Then, slowly, inevitably, like a Frankenstein's monster being built, the skeleton of a building rose from the excavation. It loomed starkly against the April sky.

Mitzi went out of her way to avoid seeing it. She stayed busy. She headed Una's new Pioneer Days Festival committee.

Butch Frost forgave her when an out-of-town buyer offered him a good price for his pasture land. Butch muttered something about bygones being bygones. Mitzi was glad.

She only hoped whoever had bought the land wasn't someone else wanting to build. Nobody had ever heard of the buyer or knew what he wanted with Butch's land. But it remained a pasture, although empty of horses.

She went out almost every evening to watch the sun set. She wished it didn't always make her think of Mac. But it did, and she supposed that these memories would simply be a part of sunsets for the rest of her life, this remembering him so sharply that it hurt.

One evening in early May she went to supper at Tilly and Una's house. She thought they had invited her to discuss some of the new projects. The real reason, she discovered, was to give her news of Barry.

The restaurant business was going badly, as everyone had predicted, but Barry had found himself the daughter of a rich oilman and was expected to marry her before summer was out.

Both Una and Tilly said the girl was only seventeen and impressionable, and that Barry had her wound firmly around his finger. She was rather plain, Tilly said, and seemed to think she was lucky that a man as handsome as Barry found her attractive. She would devote her life, her energy, and her considerable inheritance to making him happy.

Mitzi should have been depressed or angry or relieved or grateful—something. She was sure she should have felt some emotion about Barry, but she felt nothing. He had been a mistake she didn't want to dwell on. He was like a figure out of a dim and unpleasant dream. It was Mac she missed.

When she went home, she strolled out to the pasture fence. It was almost dusk, and she wanted to think, to let the breeze clear her dulled mind. The sky would be particularly spectacular tonight, she could tell, with lush ranges of cloud already starting to turn gold.

She wasn't surprised that she felt nothing about Barry's engagement. She seemed to feel little about anything these days. On the surface she remained rational, cheerful, even energetic. Underneath it was as if she were removed from reality. Events no longer seemed to touch her.

The one exception had been putting Domino out to pasture for his final years. She would always recall that day with sorrow. But she had known for a long time that it must happen. She accepted it, as she accepted Mac's loss, because she had to.

She rested one hand on the coarse wood of a fence post. The tall grass tickled her ankles. She wore the same white dress, full-skirted and sprigged with blue, that she had worn to that fateful meeting of the business association. Her hair was swept up, and a tendril blew loose in the evening breeze.

The old apple tree stood, a dark and gnarled silhouette. When a white horse cantered past it, she was so deep into her own thoughts that she hardly noticed. It might have been a horse of the imagination, a mere ghost of a horse.

But for a ghost the animal seemed surprisingly substantial. It paused at the far edge of the pasture, tossed its head then cantered back to the apple tree. It stood there, prancing and shaking its long snowy mane.

She stared harder at it. It was real, all right. And beautiful. A little Arab filly, white as milk, with the distinctive Arabian dark eyes and muzzle. The setting sun gave its sleek coat a golden tinge.

She heard footsteps in the grass behind her and tensed. A feeling so strong it left her breathless swept over her.

It was Mac. She knew it was. She knew.

But she didn't dare turn, because she might be wrong. She couldn't bear that.

But he was here. She knew. How such knowledge came to her she didn't understand. Perhaps it wasn't meant to be understood.

She was still afraid to look. Instead she squeezed her eyes shut. She stood, every muscle taut, the wind rustling her skirt.

"Aren't you going to look at me? Not even say hello?"

It was his voice. She could feel his nearness behind her as if he radiated a force to which she was hypersensitive. But she didn't dare look.

She felt his hands settle gently on her bare shoulders. In spite of the warmth of the evening and the heat of those hands, she felt a chill shake through her.

"If you're angry, I don't blame you." His breath warmed her ear. It stirred the loose strand of her hair curling against her cheek. "But look me in the eye and say it. Then maybe I'll know if there's a chance you'll forgive me. Look at me, Mitzi."

She let him turn her. But still she kept her eyes closed. It was Mac, all right. She knew his voice, she knew the sureness of his touch. She recognized the wonderful hay-and-leather scent that clung to him. But she feared letting the keenest of her senses, her sight, test his reality.

She felt his big hands frame her face. "Mitzi," he whispered roughly. "Look at me. Please."

She opened her eyes. She felt dizzy. He actually stood before her, tall, solid, slightly raw-boned. He wore a pale blue shirt, its sleeves rolled up to the elbows, and his favorite battered gray Stetson hat. An unruly lock of dark red hair hung over his forehead. He was deeply tanned, and freckles spattered his cheekbones. For a man some might consider plain, he seemed truly beautiful to her, almost painfully beautiful.

He looked down into her eyes for a long moment. "I had to come back."

She couldn't say anything. But in her silence was a question that he understood.

He nodded. "I couldn't keep my mind off you. I tried. I couldn't. Are you glad to see me?"

She nodded wordlessly. *Glad* seemed something of an understatement. She was so delighted to see him that she thought surely she must drink him in while she could, for she couldn't bear such happiness. She would dissolve in its power.

"Did you miss me at all?" he asked.

"Yes." She wanted to tell him how profoundly she had missed him, describe it in every particular, but she found it hard to get even the one word out.

He swallowed. "You've been all right? How's Dancing Sky? How's everything?"

She, too, swallowed hard. "I'm fine. Dancing Sky's going to give Polaris a run for the money. I warn you. You're going to compete against some determined people."

He stroked the dark smoothness of her hair. He smiled, albeit solemnly. "So I hear. From Spaulding. He says Polaris should bring out the best in Dancing

Sky. Thanks in part to you. Thanks in great part. He said you were something special at that meeting. That you shone out like a star.''

''I'm no star. It was rough for a while. And it'll be rough again. But you were right. We can adjust. And you were right about Barry. He sold the ranch. He left town. He's got someone else now. It's for the best.''

''I know he sold the ranch. I bought it. By proxy. So he wouldn't know.''

Her eyes widened in surprise. Surely she was dreaming. Mac couldn't really be here, and he couldn't have said such an astounding thing.

''You bought it? Why?''

''I didn't want to crush the life out of him. I just wanted you free of him. Now you are. You don't regret it?''

''I don't regret it.''

His touch was intoxicating her more than anyone's touch should do. He couldn't feel as strongly as she did, Mitzi thought, it wasn't possible. She must control herself. She stepped back slightly. ''I had enemies for a while,'' she said, trying to sound calm. ''Especially Butch Frost. But somebody bought his pasture, so even he forgave me. In his way.''

''I figured. I'm glad.''

''You figured? The pasture—?''

''I bought that, too. Spaulding arranged it. My secretary.''

She blinked up at him. He had confused her again, but the feeling was so familiar it was almost comfortable.

''You bought a pasture out in the middle of nowhere? Why?''

"For you. So it'll always stay a pasture. With apple trees and a horse or two. The way you wanted."

She didn't know what to say. She looked out at the pasture, growing more golden with each passing moment.

Nervously she clasped her hands in the folds of her full skirt. "That's your horse, then? She's beautiful."

He shook his head. He gave her the same solemn smile. "She's yours. First cousin to mine. Her name's Abilene Snow White."

"Mine?" Mitzi looked at him in bewilderment.

His hands moved to her hair. He pulled out one pin, then another, dropping them. "Let your hair down. You know how I love to touch it."

Her hair fell in a dark tumble to her shoulders. He smoothed it out and looked at her. "I talked to Judy. She told me about Domino. So I brought Snow White. If you'll have her."

Mitzi smiled up at him, touched, shaking her head. "I can't take a gift like that, Mac. It's too expensive."

"No. It's how it's supposed to be done. I endow you with my worldly goods. If you'll have me. After all I did to you."

Mitzi wanted to reach out, touch his rugged face, trace her fingers over his freckled cheekbone. But she could only stand primly, her hands still clasped. "What you did to me—" she began, uncertain what to say. She tried again. "What you did to me—"

He read her unspoken desire. He took her hand, laid it against the hard angle of his jaw. "What I did to you was high-handed. It was arrogant. You were right. I tried to play God. I saw a beautiful, spirited, giving woman, and I wanted to save her. Save you. Because you're special. I always told you that."

He took his hand from hers, reaching once more to play with a strand of her hair. Shyly she kept her fingers against his jawline, let her thumb trace his cheekbone.

"My mistake," he went on, "was not admitting I wanted you. For myself. You weren't in my plans. I hadn't expected you. Bright. Incorruptible. Honest and generous. And so desirable it's like a spear through me everytime I see you."

She nodded wordlessly. He knew, then, how it felt—how she felt. His feeling was as intense as her own.

"I thought I could play the knight," he said harshly. "Set you free and then ride off and leave you for somebody else. But I couldn't leave you. Not in my thoughts. Not for a day. Not for an hour. It sounds crazy... I left you. But I never left you."

"No," she whispered with emotion. "You didn't. You were with me, too. You were always here." She touched one hand to her heart.

He took her hand in his. "I tried to forget you. For months. Because you scared me. You with your absolute integrity and crooked smile and your hair that blows so free in the wind. It should always blow free, you know."

He gathered up a silky handful at the nape of her neck. He bent over her and kissed her, long and searchingly.

"I suppose we love each other," he murmured against her lips. "What do you think?"

"I suppose we do." Her voice shook slightly. She still wasn't certain this was happening.

He drew back, smiling. "A lot of women want a man for his money. You're the only one I know who'd like him in *spite* of it. I've wondered about dragging you into the crazy world I live in. But if you can stand it, come with me. I need you. And I think you need me.''

Again she could only nod.

''If we're together,'' he said, running his fingers through her hair, ''life might not seem so crazy. The money can be both blessing and curse. You've seen that. But I promise you, whatever it can buy, it's yours.''

''I love you,'' she answered, shaking her head and staring up at him earnestly. ''I don't care what can be bought. You're what's important. Who's important.''

''The power can be a burden,'' he went on, just as earnestly. ''You've seen that, too. I'm not really offering you such a great deal, Mitzi. A red-headed workaholic who has to fight like the devil for privacy. A life that won't be like other peoples'. Could you stand it? Can I be the prince I told you to wait for?''

She smiled, tears in her eyes. ''You were always my prince.''

''When California gets too hectic, we'll have a place here for you to come home to. We'll keep your motel standing forever, if you want to, find the best manager in the world for it. We'll fix up the old Gabler ranch, have a retreat. If that has bad memories and you'd rather have a different place, then you'll have it. But this is your pasture, forever, with all the sunsets reserved in your name. I love you, Mitzi.''

She put her arms around his neck shyly. There were things to be said, questions to be asked, plans to be made, but that was for later. For now she wanted only to taste the perfect sweetness of the moment. She raised her lips to his.

Out in the pasture the little Arab filly seemed to sense something special surging on the evening air. She began running again, simply for the joy of it. She reared at some imaginary phantom, struck at it playfully with her hooves, then cantered from it. She pranced, wild and giddy, through the swaying grass.

Mitzi didn't see. Neither did Mac. They lost themselves in each other's arms. They kissed so intently that the rest of the world turned to enchantment.

Perhaps it was only an illusion—the wind in the clouds—the breeze in the evening air—but the whole wide golden spring sky seemed to dance around them.

HARLEQUIN
Romance

Coming Next Month

THE LOVES OF A CENTURY...

Join American Romance in a nostalgic look back at the Twentieth Century—at the lives and loves of American men and women from the turn-of-the-century to the dawn of the year 2000.

Journey through the decades from the dance halls of the 1900s to the discos of the seventies ... from Glenn Miller to the Beatles ... from Valentino to Newman ... from corset to miniskirt ... from beau to Significant Other.

Relive the moments ... recapture the memories.

Look now for the CENTURY OF AMERICAN ROMANCE series in Harlequin American Romance. In one of the four American Romance titles appearing each month, for the next twelve months, we'll take you back to a decade of the Twentieth Century, where you'll relive the years and rekindle the romance of days gone by.

Don't miss a day of the CENTURY OF AMERICAN ROMANCE.

A CENTURY OF
AMERICAN ROMANCE
1900's

The women...the men...the passions...
the memories....

CAR-1

COMING SOON

DREAMSCAPE
Harlequin
ROMANCE ™

In August, two worlds will collide in four very special romance titles. Somewhere between first meeting and happy ending, Dreamscape Romance will sweep you to the very edge of reality where everyday reason cannot conquer unlimited imagination—or the power of love. The timeless mysteries of reincarnation, telepathy, psychic visions and earthbound spirits intensify the modern lives and passion of ordinary men and women with an extraordinary alluring force.

Available next month!

EARTHBOUND—Rebecca Flanders
THIS TIME FOREVER—Margaret Chittenden
MOONSPELL—Regan Forest
PRINCE OF DREAMS—Carly Bishop

DRSC